A BOOK OF SCRIPTS

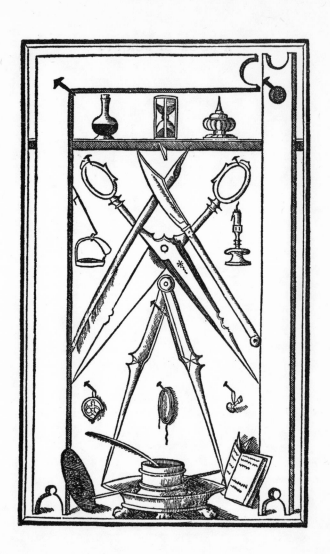

A BOOK OF SCRIPTS

by Alfred Fairbank

Faber and Faber

This edition published in 1977
by Faber and Faber Limited
3 Queen Square London WC1
Previously published in 1949 and 1968
by Penguin Books Limited Harmondsworth

—

Printed in Great Britain by
Richard Clay (The Chaucer Press) Ltd. Bungay
and John Swain and Son Ltd. London

—

—

ISBN 0 571 10876 8 (hard-bound edition)
SBN 0 571 11080 0 (Faber Paperback)

—

ACKNOWLEDGEMENTS

THE author wishes to express his gratitude for permission to reproduce the plates and figures of this book to the Vice-Prefect of the Biblioteca Apostolica Vaticana, Rome; the Directors of the Bibliothèque Nationale, Paris, the Pierpont Morgan Library, New York, and the Victoria and Albert Museum; the Trustees of the British Library, and of the National Library of Scotland, Edinburgh; the Keeper of Public Records; the Syndics of the Fitzwilliam Museum, Cambridge; the Librarians of the Bodleian Library, Oxford, and of St John's College, Cambridge; the Rector of Stonyhurst College; the Friends of the National Libraries (for Plates 2 and 3 reproduced from the Palaeographical Society's Facsimiles); the Oxford University Press; the London University Press; the Dryad Press; Blackie; Faber & Faber; Mrs James Wardrop; Mrs Irene Wellington; Miss Margaret Alexander; Miss Vera Law.

The author wishes to acknowledge the help he received from the late Professor Francis Wormald and the late Jan Tschichold. He extends his thanks to Dr R. W. Hunt, F.B.A., F.S.A., Dr A. S. Osley, and Dr Berthold L. Wolpe, R.D.I., all of whom have given him assistance.

CONTENTS

HISTORICAL SKETCH

Whence did the wond'rous mystic art arise,
Of painting SPEECH, *and speaking to the eyes?*
That we by tracing magic lines are taught,
How to embody, and to colour THOUGHT?

THE marvellous faculty of writing has led various races to attribute its origin to the gods. Assyrian, Egyptian, Chinese, Indian, and Scandinavian deities have all been held to have given man knowledge of writing. Joseph Champion in his *The Parallel or Comparative Penmanship Exemplified* (?1750) says: 'The origin of PENMANSHIP, or first invention of LETTERS, has been much controverted; but next to GOD, the Author and Giver of all science, it seems rational to think it was derived from *Adam.*' The very beginnings of our writing are now thought to be indicated by the pictures made by prehistoric man whose artistic skill is evident in caves in Spain and France. First came the drawing of a thing and then the abbreviated and conventionalized drawing used as a sign (pictograph). A later stage is when the drawing or sign represents an idea (ideograph): for instance, the sign for sun might represent day. Eventually the sign becomes a sound-symbol and indicates the sound of a word or of a syllable, and finally the sound of a letter. The last of these stages is that triumph of the mind – the invention of the alphabet, the means by which the combination of a few symbols may represent any spoken word.

The Phœnicians are said to have evolved our alphabet, with a debt to Egyptian hieroglyphics; and the Semitic alphabet, made up of consonants and written from right to left (as in modern Hebrew), was borrowed by the Greeks. The names of the first four signs of the Phœnician alphabet were: *aleph, beth, gimel,* and *daleth,* and the names of the Greek letters, obviously derivative, have no other significance than as names of letters: e.g. *alpha, beta, gamma, delta*. The word 'alphabet' comes from *alpha* and *beta*.

The Greeks added vowels, and completed the alphabet, and from writing from right to left, they wrote to the left and then to the right in successive lines (in ploughing style) and finally to the right only, as we do – a suitable arrangement for the easy movement of the right arm.

The Romans in turn adopted the alphabet, taken either directly from Greek colonists at Cumae (near Naples) or perhaps indirectly through the Etruscans, and adapted it. Plate 1 will show that, whatever may have been the influences affecting the early Latin alphabet and inscriptions, the Romans brought the design of lettering to a superb standard of quality.

In the shaping of letters the tools and materials employed encourage certain tendencies. One would expect chisel-cut strokes to be mostly straight, but the pen, gliding over an easy surface, tends to make curved strokes. The finely formed 'serifs' (the formed terminals readily identified in the letter I of Plate 1) are possibly an expression of the carver's liking for ornament, but the incidences of thicks, thins, curves, and gradations are surely vestigial traces of the use of an edged pen or a flat brush.

The Roman book-scripts that have come down to us were written in capitals (majuscules): square capitals, rustic capitals, uncials, and half-uncials. The square capitals are plainly related to the carved inscriptional letters (Plate 2). This script may have been reserved for the finest manuscripts. The usual book-hand of the Roman Empire was of rustic capitals, which are freer, compressed, and economical, and this script, first seen in a papyrus manuscript of the first century, survived until the beginning of the sixth century (Plate 3). The rustic letters have thin vertical strokes and this suggests the pen or brush may have been cut with a left-oblique edge.

Another book-hand, the uncial, to be seen in our oldest copies of the Bible, had been evolved by the fourth century and was the literary hand for fine books from the fifth to the eighth centuries. The uncial is truly a penman's letter and owes its form to the quill and to vellum – the best pen and the best writing material for a book-script. The pen makes rounded forms easily and rounded letters supplant angular ones of the earlier capitals. Uncials are shown in Plates 4, 5, 6, 9, and 11, where the characteristic shapes of ADEHM may be noted.

These three sorts of capitals belong to the family of 'formal' hands. A Roman cursive or informal handwriting was used in letters, documents, etc. (Figure 1). This cursive writing was developed from the formal capitals, but the tendency of the

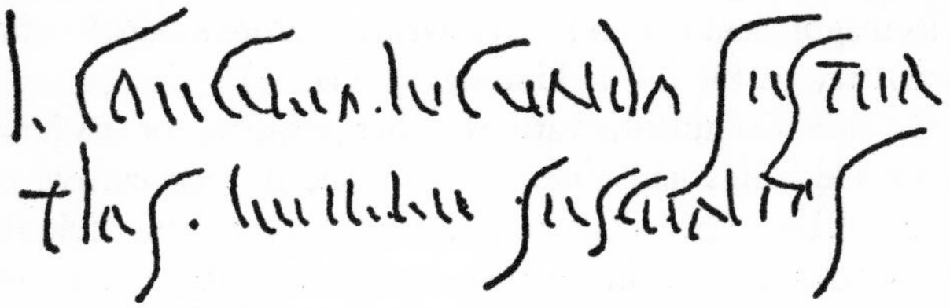

Figure 1. Roman Cursive. The words are
'L. Caecilio Iucundo sester/tios mille sescentos'.

hand when writing quickly to make the letters in a more direct and economical but less precise manner, led to considerable deviations from the capitals. Differences in writing instruments and materials cause differences in scripts. The letters produced by scratching the surface of a wax tablet will not have the same character and form as those written by quill on vellum.

The letters of the alphabet to be seen in the first three plates, with few exceptions of which Q is one, are made as if between two imaginary horizontal lines. A mixture of uncial and cursive resulted in the development of the half-uncial majuscule, and this hand marks a change towards the condition of today where the small letters fall between four imaginary horizontal lines, instead of two, because of the extensions of certain letters: e.g. b, d, f, h, k, and l, which have 'ascenders', and g, j, p. q, and y, which have 'descenders'.

St Patrick (?389–461) not only led the mission which spread Christianity in Ireland but in so doing opened up that country to the culture of Continental Europe. In the sixth and seventh centuries Ireland became a centre of art and learning, attracting Continental visitors and sending out missionaries and the Irish books and script. The eighth-century *Book of Kells* is written in Insular (Irish) half-uncials of astonishing quality. Irish monks took their culture from Iona to Northumbria, and the Anglo-Saxon book-hand developed as an insular half-uncial, rather than as a progeny of the Continental hands. The English half-uncial, or round insular hand, is seen at its magnificent best in gospels written before A.D. 698 at the monastery on the Isle of Lindisfarne (Plate 7).

On the Continent, various other regional or national minuscule hands had emerged from the Roman cursive or from a mixture of half-uncial and cursive: e.g. Visigothic (in Spain), Beneventan (in Southern Italy), and Merovingian (in France).

The history of writing is partly concerned with changes of tempo and status of scripts. A cursive hand, conditioned by economy and speed, may in time be elevated to the status and formality of a book-hand. Then, by a slackening of control, the regularized book-hand may descend to a cursive again or take on cursive characteristics.

One cannot be sure whether the Caroline minuscule (named after Charlemagne and sometimes called Carolingian) rose from a cursive or from a mixture of cursive and half-uncial, but its clear letters won for it a proud place in the history of the scripts (Plate 9). The earliest version is in the Bible written for Abbot Maurdramnus of Corbie who died in 778. Charlemagne and the Englishman, Alcuin of York (born in 735 and Abbot of the Monastery of St Martin at Tours from 796 to his death in 804) had encouraged and helped to establish this minuscule. Alcuin's revision of the Vulgate and the revival of interest in the classics during the Carolingian Renaissance led to considerable activity by scribes. The Caroline minuscule spread and particularly sensible and noble English variants of it were written in Southern England in the tenth century. Plate 10 shows the firm and clear script closely studied by Edward Johnston, and Plate 11 represents the majestic *Benedictional of St Ethelwold*,

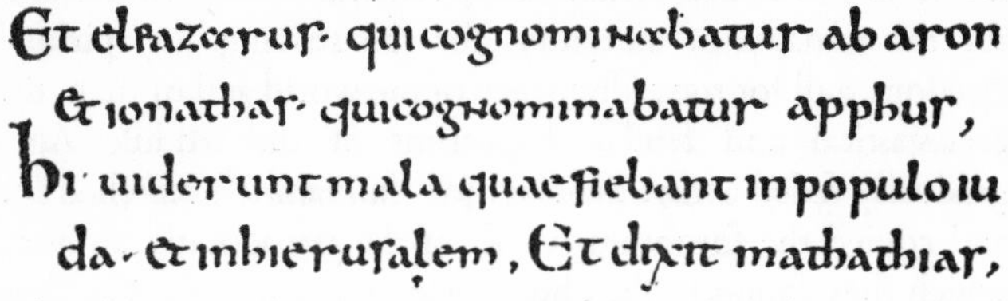

Et elfazærur· quicognominabatur abaron
  et ionathar· quicognominabatur apphur,
hr uiderunt mala quaefiebant in populo iu
da· et inhierufalem, Et dyat mathathiar,

Figure 2. From the *Maurdramnus Bible.*

remarkable also for its superb illuminating. The Caroline minuscule is still significant, for the lower-case letters in use in many parts of the world today ultimately derive from it.

The *Domesday Book*, a survey of English estates and inhabitants made by order of William the Conqueror in 1086, was written in Caroline minuscules (Plate 13).

The Gothic scripts of the Middle Ages come from the Caroline, the changed shapes of the letters being due, amongst other possible reasons, to lateral compression or to a tendency to make rounded letters somewhat angular when writing the Caroline hand too freely. It offers a striking contrast to Caroline, for, although some of the early mediaeval hands were superb, the Gothic became a precise, angular, compressed, black, ornamental letter, lacking the practicality of its clear and freer ancestor and, at its worst, lifeless and hard to read. The Gothic letters, like Gothic architecture, went through a regular process of evolution: the spirit of the Middle Ages is certainly expressed in its manuscripts as in its buildings. There are many versions of the Gothic letter, both formal and informal, but the size of this book does not allow adequate representation (Plates 16, 17, 50 and 51). In Italy the letter did not take on such angularity as in France and England (Plate 17).

But for the spreading influence of the 'New Learning', Gothic letters might normally be used in England now. During that transitional and self-conscious period which we know as the Italian Renaissance, remarkable for enthusiasm for the remains of antiquity, for the striving for spiritual freedom, and for the rediscovery of the world and of man, the ecclesiastical and feudal despotisms of the Middle Ages gradually faded away. Scholars (or 'humanists') searched for and copied the forgotten works of the classic Latin authors, which they found in the abbeys, etc., written in the Caroline hands of the eleventh to twelfth centuries. The clear writing of the classics accorded with the spirit of the 'new birth' and humanists adopted the earlier hands for their own usage. The revived Caroline hands, which we term 'humanistic', and may regard as roman, were called by the humanists *littera antiqua* for they believed them to be of classic Roman antiquity (Plates 18, 20, and 21).

Hundreds of manuscript books written in humanistic (roman) scripts in Italy in the fifteenth century have survived and there are rich collections in English libraries. Many are decorated by a style of illuminating called 'white vine', a simple form of which is shown in Plate 20. These books are in the background of the history of the art of printing, and, indeed, the credit for the invention of the roman letter is given to Poggio Bracciolini (1380–1459), whilst Niccolò Niccoli (1364–1437) has been named as the inventor of italic. Scripts of these two Florentine scholars are shown in Plates 18 and 19. (The italic script may have been a development rather than an invention, owing its cursive form to fluency and the incorporation of the diagonal joins of mediaeval cursive scripts.)

The interest of the humanists in the ruins of Rome and elsewhere led them to the carved letters of ancient inscriptions in stone, and these also were studied and used as models for fifteenth-century manuscripts, memorials, medals, and types. An interest in Roman lettering and inscriptions is also to be noted in the paintings of some Renaissance artists: for example, in those of Andrea Mantegna. Antonio Tophio, Bartolomeo San Vito, and other scribes enlivened their manuscripts by Roman capitals written in gold and colours (Plates 23 and 24). The superb Roman capitals seen in Plates 46 and 47 are authentic and the result of careful studies by G. F. Cresci nearly a century later.

Printing by movable types in the West is generally said to have been invented by Johann Gutenberg (about 1450) and to have been brought to Italy by Conrad Sweynheim and Arnold Pannartz, who set up a press in a monastery at Subiaco, near

TSI NON Dubitabam quin hanc epiſtolā nūcii fama deīq; eſſ& ipſa ſua celeritate ſupera tuq; āte ab aliis auditurus eſſes annū tertiū acc deſiderio noſtro & labori tuo:tamen exiſtimau quoq; tibi huius moleſtiæ nūcium perferri opc Nam ſuperioribus litteris:non unis:ſed plurib

Figure 3. From *Ciceronis Epistolae* printed by Nicolas Jenson in Venice, 1475. (A large initial E has been omitted.)

Rome, in 1465. The design of Gutenberg's type was taken from a formal Gothic book-hand, but the Subiaco type is nearer to the humanistic hands. The first of the types for printing used in Italy which we should call roman and recognize as being of our tradition, was that of the brothers Johann and Wendelin de Spira (Venice, 1469), but the finest roman types of the fifteenth century were those of a Frenchman, Nicolas Jenson (Venice, 1460, Figure 3), and of the famous publisher Aldus Manutius (Venice, 1495). Both these

15

excellent types have been copied for use today: the words the reader now sees are printed in the Monotype version of the Aldine type ('Monotype Bembo'). The letters owe their form to the capitals of the ancient Roman inscriptions and to the minuscules of the humanistic hands of the Italian Renaissance. There is, however, a feature of the humanistic printed lower-case letters certainly not found in the Caroline script, namely the serif such as that at the base of the letters f, h, i, l, m, n, p, q, and r. The roman minuscules written by such scribes as Poggio, Gherardo, and Sinibaldi show the Caroline terminal serifs. The rhythmical pattern and the oblique incidence of the shading speak of the pen. However, roman minuscules of the fifteenth century are found in various versions, and a dominant later style, well established in the sixteenth century, does have serifs much like those seen in Figure 3 and a vertical accent of shading. This style was subject seemingly to rules about the spacing of letters (Plates 25, 31, and 57).

The italic, the supplementary sloping type used by printers for the purposes of contrast and emphasis, is derived from a cursive variant of the revived Caroline letter and owes its simpler form to the tendency of the hand to seek the easier course and to avoid uneconomical pen-lifts. The roman n, for example, has a rounded arch, and to make a satisfactory arch of this shape one must lift the pen on completing the first down stroke. If the pen is not lifted and the arch springs from the very base of the stroke, then the arch is likely to be narrowed, if not pointed, such as in the italic *n*. A difference, therefore, between roman and italic lower-case types is that one derives from a formal hand and the other from a cursive. Fluency is helped by the use of linking joins, particularly those of a diagonal kind, but not all letters are joined. The slope and compression of italic letters are also cursive characteristics. The clarity and convenience of the humanistic cursive hand led to its use both as a book-script and for correspondence. Its adoption in the Papal chancery for the writing of Briefs must have contributed to its acceptance in

European countries (Plate 32). The script came to be termed *littera de brevi* or *littera cancellaresca* in Italy.

The free italic was given precise or 'set' form in type when Aldus Manutius Romanus published a *Virgil* in Venice in 1501, the first of his small editions of the classics. This type includes many letters coupled by diagonal joins and other

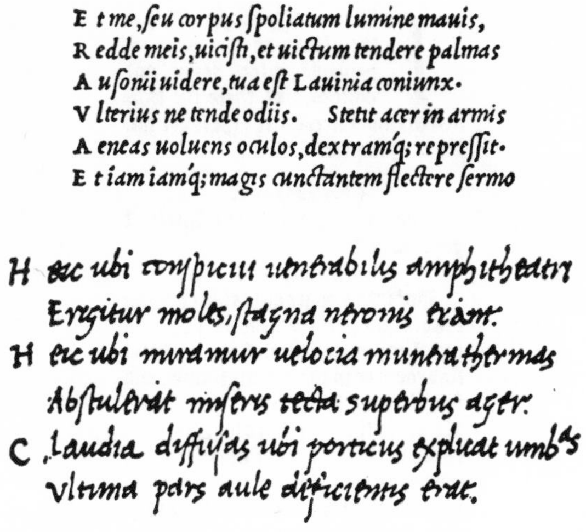

Figure 4. From a *Virgil* printed by Aldus in Venice in 1501, contrasted with the book-hand of Pomponio Leto below.

ligatures: a sign of currency in whatever was the parent script (Figure 4).

The significance of the relationship between scripts and printing types is that printing has preserved Renaissance letter-forms and has set a standard of legibility from which it is well that contemporary penmen should not stray too far.

In 1522 Ludovico degli Arrighi (Vicentino), a writer of apostolic briefs as well as a scribe, printer, and designer of italic types, produced the first writing manual to deal with italic handwriting, at the clamour of his friends. The pages of *La Operina*, printed from engraved wood-blocks, offer instruction in writing as well as exemplify the beautiful *cancellaresca* hand (Plate 28). Arrighi's second book, *Il Modo*,

PRECEPTES OF
WRITING.

The writer must prouide him these seuē: paper, incke, pen, penknife, ruler, deske, and dustbox, of these the thrée first are most necessarie, the foure latter very requisite.

Choyse of paper.

The whitest, finest, and smothest paper is best.

To make inke.

Put into a quart of water two ounces of right gumme Arabick, fiue, ounces of galles, and thrée of coprzas. Let it stād couered in the warme sunne, and so will it the sooner prooue good incke. To boyle the sayd stuffe together a little vpon the fire would make it more spédy for your writyng: but ȳ vnboyled yeldeth a fayrer glosse, & lōger indureth. In stead of water wine were best for this purpose. Refresh your incke with wine, or vineger, whē it wareth thicke,

Figure 5. From *The Petie Schole* by Francis Clement. 1587.

with plates engraved in Venice in 1523, shows a variety of hands and alphabets, including models for a commercial hand, a notary's script, and for Papal Bulls and Briefs, etc. Arrighi's italic book-script, illuminated in the style of Attavante, is represented in Plate 30 and the Papal Brief of Plate 32 was probably written by him. The very popular writing-book of G. A. Tagliente, containing even more scripts and alphabets, appeared in 1524 (Plate 29). In 1540 G. B. Palatino published a very treasury of scripts (Plate 34). Similar books began to appear in other countries, namely France, Switzerland, Spain (Plates 44 and 45), the Netherlands (Plate 35), Germany (Plate 36), and England.

The first writing-book printed in England is *A Booke Containing Divers Sortes of Hands* by Jean de Beauchesne and John Baildon (Plates 49–51). Two other books show specimens of Beauchesne's penmanship, namely *A Newe Booke of Copies 1574* and *The Petie Schole* by Francis Clement, 1587. Beauchesne's book shows 'as well the English as French secretarie, Italian, Roman, Chancelry and court hands'.

The *cancellaresca* hand, traditionally held to have been introduced into the English Court by Petrus Carmelianus, Latin Secretary to Henry VII, was accepted slowly, but it found in Roger Ascham (1515–68) an influential and fine practitioner. Ascham, a pioneer of English prose, who wrote 'English matter in the English tongue for English men', taught the italic hand to Edward VI and Elizabeth I and was Latin Secretary to Mary. The Lady Elizabeth under his tuition became a very able writer, and if in later life she confessed to a 'skrating hand' it is not uncommon to find departures from early performances and standards. Ascham's influence is doubtless behind the most accomplished and graceful writing of Bartholomew Dodington (1536–95), Regius Professor of Greek at Cambridge (Plate 42).

The influence on Ascham was Sir John Cheke, the first Regius Professor of Greek at Cambridge, who was said by John Strype to have brought to Cambridge University 'fair and graceful Writing by the Pen, as he wrote an excellent accurate hand himself' (Plate 40). Numerous letters addressed by Cambridge scholars to Elizabeth I or to Lord Burleigh written in fine italic style are preserved in the Lansdowne papers in the British Museum and in State Papers in the Public Record Office.

From being a hand of the Court and of the travelled, the italic became one of the scripts of the well-educated and of scriveners. The principal hand was 'secretary', a Gothic script. The small sloped secretary, which Billingsley described as 'the onely usuall hand of England for dispatching of all manner of business', was considered to be a speedier hand and one more suitable for ordinary usage than italic. The two hands were sometimes mixed, and in various ways: for instance, when writing in secretary not only might words be put in italic writing for emphasis but also italic letter-forms might be introduced in the words.

The writing-book of G. A. Hercolani marks the introduction of a new feature, for the examples are reproduced by engraved copperplate instead of by engraved wood-block (Plate 52). Hercolani's excellent engraved examples are close to handwriting and are free of too great an angularity. In time, however, the engraver's needle, scoring the surface of the polished plate, tended to give to the pupil the letter-forms proper to the burin rather than to the quill, and to lead the writing masters to the use of a needle-pointed flexible pen.

Another factor also pointing in the direction of decay is that the bulbous beginning of *bbl*, etc., which is quite discreet in Hercolani's specimens and may have originated in a natural turning movement of the pen, became an obtrusive decorative feature of the Italian hand without contributing to legibility or speed. Decoration for its own sake is a doubtful quality in a correspondence hand. The style was known as *cancellaresca testegiata*.

Martin Billingsley's book *The Pens Excellencie* (1618), dedicated to Prince Charles, who was a pupil of the master, shows secretary, bastard secretary, Roman, Italian, court, and chancery hands. Of Roman, to him a hand not much different from Italian, he writes bluntly that 'it is conceived to be the easiest hand that is written with Pen, and to be taught in the shortest time: Therefore it is usually taught to Women . . .'. Another contemporary, John Davies of Hereford, poet and writing master to Henry, Prince of Wales, is represented by *The Writing Schoolemaster* (?1631) which appeared some years

20

after his death. His graceful hand, like that of Billingsley, is marred by the weighting of ascenders and descenders (Plate 54).

Edward Cocker (1631–76) combined the arts of penman and engraver and produced over two dozen writing-books engraved on copper, brass, and silver plates. Among the enthusiastic titles are *Pen's Experience, Pen's Transcendencie, Pen's Triumph, Pen's Celerity, Pen's Facility, Multum in Parvo or the Pen's Gallantrie* (Plates 58 and 59). A number of the English writing masters were contemptuous, aggressive, and vain, issuing challenges and allowing their portraits and excessive praise to appear in their books; but their devotion to their craft and recognition of their eminent predecessors and even of their contemporaries are compensating qualities. Joseph Champion in his *The Parallel* writes that

Mr Edward Cocker, a voluminous author, led on by lucre, let in an inundation of copy-books and these followed by others, either vile imitators of pirates in PENMANSHIP, had almost rendered the art contemptuous, when col. *John Ayres*, a disciple of Mr *Topham's*, happily arose to check this mischievous spirit (which was about the year 1690) and he actually began the reformation of LETTERS, and introduced the mixed round hands, since naturalised and improved amongst us: he was indefatigable and wrote all hands, more especially the law-hands, finely; nor is it any diminution of our CHARACTERS who survive him, to own that the colonel was our common father, who so magnificently carried the glory of *English* PENMANSHIP far beyond his predecessors.

Colonel John Ayres, who produced eleven copy-books between 1680 and 1700 (Plate 62), has wrongly been given credit for the introduction of the italic hands in England; he introduced the French Italienne-Bastarde or 'à la Model Round-hand'. Two important French writing-books, doubtless well known to English writing masters, were Lucas Materot's *Les Œuvres* (Avignon, 1608) and Louis Barbedor's *Les Écritures Financière, et Italienne-Bastarde* (Paris, 1647). Materot is described by Bickham as the Darling of the Ladies because of the elegant Italian script presented as *Lettre facile à imiter pour les femmes* (Figure 6). Champion says of Barbedor that 'his performances were peculiarly daring, free and grand', and certainly the brilliant flourished displays of his large folios seem almost to take calligraphy into the sphere of non-functional art (Plate 56). Other influences, bearing on Ayres

Figure 6. Lucas Materot's *Lettre facile à imiter pour les femmes.*

and his immediate successors and freely acknowledged, were the Dutch Masters, and particularly van den Velde (Plate 53) and Perlingh.

An anonymous copy-book titled *Young Clerks Assistant* (1733) shows an Italian hand and states it to be a narrower and lighter letter than the round hand, though otherwise related, and to be intended for the Ladies, whilst the round hand was for the Young Clerks and was plainly a business hand.

The development of the round hand was advanced by the considerable school of penman called forth by commercial necessity during the early years of the eighteenth century; significant members were George Shelley, Charles Snell, Ralph Snow, Robert More, John Clark, and George Bickham the Elder (Plates 63 to 65). When, in 1710, George Shelley secured the position of Master to the Writing School of Christ's Hospital there were over four hundred pupils. Bickham's *The Universal Penman*, issued in parts, contains not only 212 engraved plates, $16\frac{1}{2} \times 10\frac{1}{2}$ ins., but also presents the scripts of twenty-five penmen. English sea-borne trade was expanding, and handwriting and accounting had gained a new significance as Dutch commerce declined in importance. The leadership in writing had passed in the seventeenth century from the Italians to the French and Dutch, but the English running hand (taught often by writing masters who also taught 'accompts') now began to follow English exports and to spread about the Continent, and eventually to find a place in the writing-books of Paris, Cologne, Barcelona, etc.

During the early years of the eighteenth century the head-line copy-book appeared. An advertisement in a copy of Snell's *The Art of Writing* is of a 'Quarto Book to write in, with a Printed Copy at the Top of Each Leaf. Price 1s.'

The copy-books of the second half of the eighteenth century and those of the nineteenth century show hands of the Snell and Bickham tradition, but rather more direct in structure and with less decoration than Snell would have sanctioned. The hair-line is often exceedingly fine and the shading called for carefully controlled pressures. Sometimes the letters are very large, a down stroke being as much as three inches long. The Running Hand of John Seally of about 1770 has all letters joined and with loops for the purpose and he was not above linking words.

James Henry Lewis (Plate 66) and Joseph Carstairs (Plate 67) both taught that the right hand should be lightly supported by the tip of the little finger and that the forearm should be at liberty and move easily. Lewis claimed George IV, the Emperor of Russia, the King of Prussia, the Duke of Wellington, Lord Byron, Sir Walter Scott, and many other 'exalted characters' among his patrons, and also that Carstairs became a pupil of his under the fictitious name of Robert Drury. Carstairs dedicated one of his books to the Duke of Kent and another to the Duke of Sussex. The Carstairian System of Writing as taught by Benjamin Foster in New York (1830) had much influence on American commercial handwriting.

Vere Foster (1819–1900) arranged for the emigration at his own expense of many thousands of destitute Irish to the United States. His first copy-book, published in Ireland in 1868, was intended to help Irish children who would otherwise be handicapped in America by their lack of education. He was not an expert penman, and Plate 69 is of a model

23

written under his guidance, from the copy-book used by the author when 14.

William Morris (1834–96), poet and artist-craftsman, who, as early as 1856, had produced illuminations in the mediaeval manner, was much occupied during the period from 1870 to 1876 in making a series of illuminated manuscripts and during this time began to study handwriting as a fine art (Plate 70). He owned a volume made up of four Italian writing-books of the sixteenth century and is known to have studied Arrighi's italic model. Doubtless he prepared the way for Edward Johnston and his school.

Edward Johnston (1872–1944) turned from the study of medicine to an intense research into the principles of design of manuscript books and the formal book-hands. He was advised as to the best models to study by the late Sir Sydney Cockerell, who as a young man had been secretary to William Morris. Johnston taught formal writing and illuminating at the London Central School of Arts and Crafts from 1899 to 1912 and at the Royal College of Art, also in London, from 1901. Enjoying a rare combination of gifts and abilities, he was able to bring to the craft, so debased by the Victorian penman and illuminator, a noble sense of design, the attitude and competence of the true artist–craftsman, and great qualities of intellect and character. Although the sum of his works is not large, yet by their excellence and by his inspiring teaching he has had a considerable influence, abroad as well as in this country. Among his pupils were the late Eric Gill and all those members of the Society of Scribes and Illuminators who are not pupils of his pupils. Mrs Irene Wellington and Miss Margaret Alexander have contributed examples of book-hands to this book (Plates 76 and 77) which at once show the grace and skill of their work and the standards of the Johnstonian school.

Edward Johnston's classic book *Writing and Illuminating, and Lettering*, first published in 1906 and reprinted numerous times, taught how to cut a quill, how to write the half-uncial hand, how to design and illuminate manuscript books and broadsides, etc., etc. In his portfolio of cards, *Manuscript and Inscription Letters*, he offered modernized versions of square capitals, rustic capitals, uncials, half-uncials, Caroline, roman and italic hands. Later he taught his students a Gothicized italic hand he had developed over the years from the tenth-century Winchester hand (Plate 72). Formal calligraphy had been taught also in the first quarter of this century in Austria by Rudolf von Larisch (1856–1934) and in Germany by Anna Simons (1871–1951) and Rudolf Koch (1874–1934) (Plate 75).

Johnston published no models of ordinary handwriting for schools, but at the annual Conference of London Teachers in January 1913 he gave an address on Penmanship in which he suggested an *ideal* course. Children might begin with Roman capitals and their origins (tracing with styles and wax tablets the passage of the capital into the skeleton small letter). This is to be followed by the practice of a half-uncial hand, then by a Caroline hand, and finally by the development of the Caroline hand into the italic. London schools began experimenting (but, it seems, without consulting Johnston), and print-script, consisting of letters made of straight lines, circles, and parts of circles, and having some relationship to Johnston's skeleton letters, began to replace the hands of the copperplate tradition in the infants' schools.

print-script

There was a seeming economy in having to learn but one alphabet for both reading and writing, and enthusiasm was felt for the simplicity of the system. Unfortunately print-script does not develop naturally into a running hand. What the reformers had failed to learn was the lesson taught by Renaissance history, namely that the Roman letter is one written with pen-lifts and that its fluent counterpart is italic. Therefore, instead of infants being presented with a model that is not designed for fluency and which they will have to abandon, it would have been sensible to teach a simple italic hand as a first stage (Figure 7). There is virtue in the educational principle of starting as one intends to go on.

Before Edward Johnston had begun to teach, Mrs M. M. Bridges had issued her models in *A New Handwriting for Teachers* (1898). Her beautiful script owes a debt to the hands of the Italian Renaissance, which she acknowledged, but it is none the less her own (Plate 71).

In 1916 the late Graily Hewitt (1864–1952), a pupil of Edward Johnston, whose illuminated manuscript books are in cathedrals as well as on collectors' shelves, presented a cursive script for use in schools in his booklet *Handwriting: Everyman's Handicraft*. This model (Plate 78) was founded on those given in the writing-books of the sixteenth century and of Palatino and Lucas in particular. In a later book of the same title (1938), Mr Hewitt, with a view to speed, showed how certain letters could be modified to admit continuity of the running line, and to subordinate letters of the alphabet to a wave-like (counter-clockwise) action.

Another reformer was the late Marion Richardson who produced in 1928 the *Dudley Writing Cards*, an approximate

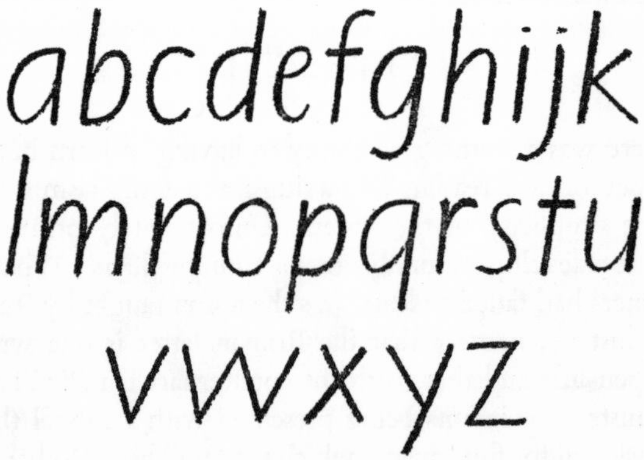

abcdefghijk
lmnopqrstu
vwxyz

Figure 7. Alphabet for infants from *Beacon Writing Book No. 1.*

and simple italic style written with broad pens, and, ten years later, her *Writing and Writing Patterns: Teachers' Book*. The later models, largely founded on writing patterns (Figure 8). indicate a changed attitude, namely that the child's first pen should write as nearly as possible as a pencil writes (Plate 79).

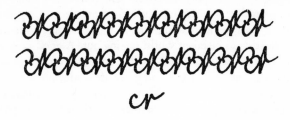

Figure 8. From *Writing and Writing Patterns* by Marion Richardson.

The italic model in the last plate is from *The Dryad Writing Cards*. The principles of design and teaching of this hand are explained in *A Handwriting Manual* (Faber & Faber). In the *Beacon Writing Books* (Ginn), made in association with Charlotte Stone and Winifred Hooper, the author's later versions of the italic hand are offered in developing styles, ranging from one claimed to be simpler than the print-script indicated on page 25 to one suitable for children, when a pen is first used, as well as for adults. The pen used was a straight-edged metal stub suitable for fast writing. The hand, of course, has some relationship to the italic of the sixteenth century.

Since this book was first produced in the King Penguin series in 1949 a considerable interest in italic handwriting has arisen. A Society for Italic Handwriting has been formed which has rapidly recruited a large and international membership and issues a quarterly journal. Another organization is the Mercator Society (Holland). Notable leaders overseas are Paul Standard and Lloyd Reynolds (U.S.A.), Chris Brand, J. and W. N. Schalkwijk (Holland), and Bent Rohde (Denmark).

Many copy-books written in various versions of the italic hand are now on the market. Numerous schools have adopted the hand and find it superior to other systems and well-liked by children.

The copy-book or set of writing-cards, written by a skilled penman without consideration of speed, displays the handwriting style in a precise version. The models are of a 'set' hand, a product of discipline but without freedom. They show how to start to learn, but, like a sign-post, they indicate the direction to be taken whilst staying put. A good personal hand is when self-discipline and freedom are reconciled, and legibility, character, speed, and grace are achieved.

One writes by a system of movements involving touch. The cinematograph can show the pen's motions as well as its track, and so future handwriting-reformers may have more impressive means of teaching handwriting than by copybooks, which are often offset by the teacher's writing on the blackboard. Loop films showing the action of writing and repeated as often as required would teach the movements producing the shapes and prove a new and valuable visual aid.

PENS

The historic scripts to be seen in the plates fall mainly into two categories: they are written with an edged pen or with a flexible pointed pen. The book-hands are in the first category and the copperplate-hands in the second.

The edged pen may be a quill, a reed, or (today) a metal pen, and the edge may be straight or oblique. The oblique-edged pen used for some book-hands has the shorter part of the nib on the right-hand side of the split. The strokes naturally produced by the edged pen (i.e. when writing without pressure on the nib) are a thick stroke as wide as the pen's edge, a thin stroke (hair-line) at right angles to the thick stroke, and intermediate thicknesses and gradations governed by the direction of the stroke. Curved strokes have gradations of mathematical regularity. The downstroke is rarely the thickest stroke, and the angle of the thick (or thin) stroke varies between scripts. In a formal hand the strokes are pulled strokes fitted together with many pen-lifts, so:

ondg ondg

In a cursive hand these letters would be made without lifting the pen and the strokes would be pulled, pushed, and sidled.

The eighteenth- and nineteenth-century commercial hands require a flexible pointed pen held so that the downstroke, made by the flexing of fingers and thumb, is the result of a pressure that splays the points of the pen. Seemingly the aim

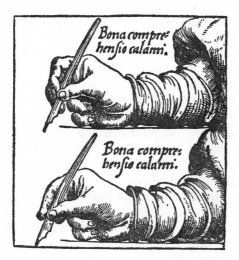

Figure 9. From *Libellus valde doctus* by Urban Wyss. Zürich, 1549.
(Also shown in *A Newe Booke of Copies 1574.*)

29

was to imitate the strokes the engraving tool produced. Therefore, it could be said that the pen was not master in its own house. A threat to good handwriting today is the 'ball-point' (an ink-pencil rather than a pen!).

The hair-line of the early italic is made by a sideways movement of an edged pen, whilst the hair-line of the copperplate-hand results from a release of pressure on the nib. Both kinds of upstrokes are produced by natural and easy movements. Not so natural and easy are the uniform gradations of the copperplate-hands. The edged pen is rarely pointed to the right shoulder: a position more suitable for exerting pressure.

The left-hander who learns the italic hand is recommended to use a left-oblique nib or one of the left-hand fountain pens which has a point bent towards the left at an angle near the point.

LEGIBILITY

What are the virtues, combining function and delight, which we may look to see expressed in the hands shown in the plates? Obviously legibility should come first, and character, economy, and grace follow close behind. The degrees and indeed standards of legibility vary considerably. When reading handwriting, we do not expect the ease we enjoy in reading a printed book. What is more important than great ease in reading is that what is written can be read. Robert Bridges held that 'true legibility consists in the *certainty of deciphering*' and that points to every letter being of distinctive and recognizable form.

An indifferent penman will complain of the writing of another poor writer, but this may be not so much that he fails to see his own shortcomings as that legibility depends so much upon what one is used to reading. One's own bad writing is more familiar than the other fellow's scrawl.

Pleasing appearance, as well as speed, sometimes conflicts

with easy legibility. The Gothic book-hands may make a noble and rich pattern, but they lack clarity.

Naturally in a collection of historical scripts and alphabets there are certain to be archaic features. We no longer use the long s (ʃ) in England, and there are other strange characters and signs in the ancient hands that disturb our sense of clarity or legibility because we are not accustomed to them. Abbreviations are numerous in many mediaeval manuscripts.

ECONOMY AND SPEED

The *Virgil* written in the careful and complicated square capitals some fifteen hundred years ago (Plate 2) suggests a time when the flying hours had little significance for the scribe. Yet in the same period the time-saving Roman cursive was being dashed down. It is inevitable that means of economy will be found to reduce the penman's task. Economy will not only modify scripts to save the labour of writing but will also save material by a reduction in size of letters, or by lateral compression, or close spacing.

The tug-of-war between economy (as a time-saver) and legibility appears again and again in the history of writing. Speed may in time change a script, but the instinct to write legibly and with discipline and care results in the development of a new script. The fifteenth-century Florentine humanists developed the formal Roman hand from the Caroline hands (probably of the eleventh or twelfth centuries) and also invented the informal or cursive italic. The splendid italic of Ludovico degli Arrighi of Vicenza is a current hand, shaped by speed and fit for rapid use (Plate 28). It has, however, a set form: which is to say the model is not itself freely and quickly written but is a *copy-book* cursive italic, executed carefully and slowly to make intentions clear. Amphiareo's fine model (Plate 37), is not, however, a pure cursive. An increase in legibility is procured by formal methods: the m, for example, is made with two pen-lifts, and joins are excluded. The italic book-script of Arrighi (Plate 30) is a set hand not intended, of course, as a model for a current hand. Manuscript books were made and valued for many years after the invention of printing.

A characteristic of cursive writing is a tendency for the pen to retain contact with the paper or at least to reduce the number of pen-lifts during the progress of the hand across the sheet. Arrighi says that a, c, d, f, i, k, l, m, n, s, t, and u may be joined to the letter that follows, but that b, e, g, h, o, p, q, r, x, y, and z should not (Plate 28). Whether to join or not he leaves to the judgement of the writer. Van den Velde's flourished script, published in 1605 and shown in Plate 53, has few pen-lifts and, moreover, some words are connected. Charles Snell's advice is to 'perform as much of a Word as you can in one *continued* Stroke'. Joseph Carstairs's exercise in Plate 67 is one of continuity. In print-script, however, there are no joins and nothing about the letters to suggest how they may be joined. Is not Arrighi nearer the happy mean? There is surely more freedom in lifting the pen when letters do not easily join or when the hand of the writer needs to be readjusted as it moves to the right.

CALLIGRAPHY

Calligraphy is handwriting considered as an art. Figure 10 shows how a tenth-century Chinese calligrapher expressed thunder and lightning by the form of the characters. Painting, in China, has a close relationship to calligraphy, and calligraphy to painting. If an English calligrapher finds himself writing out a poem about clouds he will not endeavour to make his letters cloud-like, nor will he try to express in his calligraphy a mood created by the poem or the spectacle of clouds. Certainly the objective patterning of his writing may evoke some feeling in the beholder, say of nobility, vitality, serenity, etc. Indeed, his writing may be serene when he is transcribing words intended to create a sense of terror and yet not be out of keeping. The Chinese calligraphers are accorded greater artistic honour than that due to Western calligraphers, but they do not enjoy the simplicities of an alphabet.

Figure 10. Specimen of Chinese calligraphy (10th century A.D.) expressing thunder and lightning. From *Background to Chinese Art* by H. G. Porteus. Faber & Faber. 1935.

The Western calligrapher, guiding his pen to form legible words, produces a fine pattern and design, and in his writing we may see unity, good form, and good arrangement. Being a craftsman, his liking for tools, materials, and methods will also be in evidence. His aim is to produce a thing of beauty and he will be 'writing-conscious' whilst working. The ephemeral note, beginning 'Dear John' or 'My dear Joan', from a person whose pleasure is in a good hand, will also doubtless be written with some writing-consciousness (with, say, half an eye on appearance), and though of modest worth, when appreciated for its grace and authenticity, may rightly have a claim to be regarded as calligraphy though not intended to be a work of art.

Unity, an essential virtue, includes affinity of letter-forms to each other, harmony of style, and consistency of rhythmical stress of strokes and spacing. Unity is quickly apprehended, and indeed we may see the uniformity of the textual column before we focus our eyes upon the words. For legibility, the letters of the alphabet must be sufficiently individual to be easily recognized and yet must have affinity: a reconciliation of difference and likeness. The degree of affinity is closer between some letters than others, yet there is even a relationship between (say) an s and all the rest of a good alphabet through size, proportion, and character of stroke. The family likenesses of written letters are partly an expression of penmanship, for the hand tends to limit the several movements it makes in the almost automatic act of writing, and to progress in set courses. In writing *a*, *c*, *e*, and *d*, for instance, there are somewhat similar (counter-clockwise) motions involved. Charles Snell regarded i, o, u, h, and y as the leading letters of the round hand and relates all the other members of the alphabet to one or two of these letters. Thomas Weston of Greenwich in his *Copy Book* (1726) showed an alphabet of minuscules, each letter of which was based upon the form of the letter *o*. J. H. Lewis, possibly influenced by an American penman, John Jenkins, unified the alphabet and simplified teaching (too much, perhaps, for letters are entities) by building up letters with a few elements (Plate 66).

Eric Gill shrewdly remarked in his *Autobiography:* 'You don't draw an A and then stand back and say: there, that gives you a good idea of an A as seen through an autumn mist.' Another comment he made is that letters are not pictures of things but things. Well, letters are both entities and elements of words. The letters of Plates 1, 2, and 3, show entitative letters, standing clear of their neighbours, and they are rather more elements of the line-pattern than of words. The scripts of Poggio, Gherardo, and Sinibaldi are clearly elements of words by the bunching of letters (Plates 18, 20, and 21), whilst the letters of the italic and copperplate hands, linked by joins, are even more the component parts of words. The examples in Plates 25, 31, and 57 have letters which are as much entities as elements of words, and in this respect closer to roman printing types.

The consistent incidence of thicks, thins, and gradations of strokes makes for harmony; and another important factor in creating unity in the script is the regular spacing of letters, words, and lines. In the writing masters' models we may look for equal spacing of letters (or the appearance of it), whilst in free individual hands the rhythmical spacing would be governed rather more by the fingers than the eyes and be less regular.

Not only should letters go well together and belong, but the letters and words and the inscription as a whole should have good construction and form. Included in form will be pen-character. Edward Johnston's view was that 'It is the broad nib that gives the pen its constructive and educational value. It is essentially the letter-making tool. . . . It may therefore be relied on largely to determine questions of form in letters. . . . In fact a broad-nibbed pen actually controls the hand of the writer and will create alphabets out of their skeletons, giving harmony and proportion and character to the different letters.' The roundness of the script in Plate 7 and the narrowness of the italic in Plate 29 are each to some extent an expression of a certain sort of pen held and moved in a certain way. Form also includes proportion: for example, a P should not be as wide as a D, for the two bows should have some relation in shape. Letterers often tend to lay down geometrical rules for the shaping of alphabets and particularly of capitals. Geometry, of course, may be allowed to give helpful hints, and the calligrapher is at an advantage if he has an image in his mind of the desired alphabet, but he writes freely and cannot, therefore, achieve perfected geometrical form.

Edward Cocker in his *Pen's Transcendencie* confessed that his Italian Hand 'wholly depends on the Eye-charming Form of an oval'. To some the o that is eye-charming is round

(Roman) and to others angular (Gothic). (For quite other reasons than charm, an oval seems right for a cursive hand.) Often a preference will be expressed for Roman (static and clear) rather than for italic (dynamic and elegant) and *vice versa*. Some letters of an alphabet are much more likeable as shapes than others. A B C D E F G are possibly preferred by readers as more pleasing forms than T U V W X Y Z. Letters

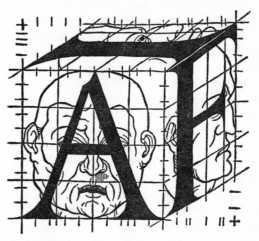

Figure 11. From *Champ Fleury* by Geofroy Tory. Paris, 1529.
Letters related to geometrical and human proportions.

must be simple in form where there is much to be read or reading will be tedious. The printer expects of his book-types a high standard of unobtrusive service, for they should not distract the reader by calling attention to their appearance, however delightful. A piece of calligraphy, being a work of art, fails if it does not evoke an immediate appreciation of its beauty.

A good letter often shows an architectural quality e.g. consider how firmly built are the letters M and m. The slight forward slope of the early italic seems constructionally sound and yet at the same time smacks of movement and fluency.

The lines of an inscription could be thought of as horizontal bands of pattern. If the lines are well spaced, and in most of the examples they are, the ascenders and descenders add a fortuitous and secondary patterning in the spaces between the strips (see Plates 37 and 42).

The arrangement of lettering provides an opportunity for the fit and skilful disposal of the elements in the well-proportioned space. If the space is the page of an early book, the outer margin will be greater than the inner one and the bottom margin greater still. Colour may add contrast and brightness. Contrast can also be given by a script that is larger, smaller, blacker, or finer, or, if good judgement is used, by a hand that is different.

Illuminating covers a wide range of artistic work, from the simple decoration of initial letters to the gloriously patterned borders surrounding the textual column and the precious miniature painting. Allied to heraldry by the use of colours and style of design, it occasionally incorporates the arms (and portraits) of patrons (Plate 30 shows the arms of Henry VIII). English draughtsmanship is shown to great advantage in such books as the *Benedictional of St Ethelwold*, the twelfth-century Winchester Bible and the famous Psalters of East Anglia produced in the early fourteenth century before the Black Death. Contemporary calligraphers of the Johnston school are often also illuminators.

A decorative feature of the folios of copperplate copy-books out-running discretion was the flourishing known to the writing masters as 'striking' or 'command of hand'. The desire of the penmen to shine by examples of amazing skill led them to performances that made writing subsidiary to ornament. In *Pen's Transcendencie* Edward Cocker framed an inscription of seven lines with an intricate interlaced pattern that entailed the pen-stroke looping and twirling many hundreds of times: the whole thing a crinkum-crankum. Snell in *The Art of Writing* protests against the wild fancies of some of 'our late Authors, who have made *Owls*, *Apes*,

Monsters, and *sprig'd Letters,* so great a Part of their Copy-Books'. This reaction from 'a whimsical Humour' developed, and in 1766 Ambrose Serle advises his students that 'a Piece of good Penmanship is its own best Ornament. It will defy Criticism, without the borrowed trappings of the fanciful Pen and has native Beauty sufficient to charm, without Circumscriptions or Additions of any kind.'

Figure 12. Latin alphabet from *Alphabet de dissemblables sortes de lettres*
by de la Rue. Paris. *c.* 1560.
(Also shown in *A Newe Booke of Copies 1574.*)

Figure 13. Greek alphabet from *Alphabet de dissemblables sortes de lettres*
by de la Rue. Paris. *c.* 1560.

SELECTED BIBLIOGRAPHY

Edward Clodd, *The Story of the Alphabet*. Hodder & Stoughton. 1900.

A. C. Moorhouse, *Writing and the Alphabet*. Cobbett Press. 1946.

David Diringer, *Writing*. Thames & Hudson. 1962.

I. J. Gelb, *A Study of Writing*. University of Chicago Press. 1952. Revised 1963.

B. L. Ullman, *Ancient Writing and its Influence*. Harrap. 1932.

Edward Maunde Thompson, *Introduction to Greek and Latin Palaeography*. Oxford University Press. 1912.

Hermann Degering, *Lettering*. Ernest Benn. 1929, 1965.

E. A. Lowe, *Codices Latini Antiquiores*. Parts I to XI. Oxford University Press. 1934–66.

E. A. Lowe, *English Uncial*. Oxford University Press. 1960.

E. A. Lowe, 'Handwriting'. Included in *The Legacy of the Middle Ages*. Oxford University Press. 1926.

N. R. Ker, English Manuscripts in the Century after the Norman Conquest. Oxford University Press. 1960.

R. W. Hunt, 'Palaeography'. Article in *Chambers Encyclopedia*. Pergamon Press, 1950.

Julian Brown, 'Palaeography'. Article in *The Encyclopedia Britannica*. 1966.

Jan Tschichold, *An Illustrated History of Writing and Lettering*. Zwemmer, London. 1947.

Jan Tschichold, *Meisterbuch der Schrift*. Otto Maier Verlag, Ravensburg. 1952.

Two Thousand Years of Calligraphy. Illustrated Catalogue compiled by Dorothy E. Miner, Victor I. Carlson, and P. W. Filby of an exhibition in Baltimore. Walters Art Gallery, Baltimore. 1965.

B. L. Ullman, *The Origin and Development of Humanistic Script*. Edizioni di Storia e Letteratura, Rome. 1960.

Alfred Fairbank and Berthold Wolpe, *Renaissance Handwriting: An Anthology of Italic Scripts*. Faber & Faber. 1960.

Alfred Fairbank and R. W. Hunt, *Humanistic Script of the Fifteenth and Sixteenth Centuries*. Bodleian Library, Oxford. 1960.

Alfred Fairbank and Bruce Dickins, *The Italic Hand in Tudor Cambridge*. Cambridge Bibliographical Society Monograph No. 5. Bowes & Bowes. 1963.

James Wardrop, *The Script of Humanism*. Oxford University Press. 1963.

Stanley Morison, 'Early Humanistic Script and the First Roman Type'. Article in *The Library*, Fourth Series, Vol. XXIV, Nos. 1 and 2. 1943.

39

Hilary Jenkinson, *The Later Court Hands in England, from the Fifteenth to Seventeenth Century.* Cambridge University Press. 1927.

N. Denholm-Young, *Handwriting in England and Wales.* University of Wales Press. 1954.

L. C. Hector, *The Handwriting of English Documents.* Edward Arnold. 1958. Revised 1966.

C. E. Wright, *English Vernacular Hands from the Twelfth to the Fifteenth Centuries.* Oxford University Press. 1960.

Sir Ambrose Heal, *The English Writing Masters and Their Copy-Books.* Introduction by Stanley Morison. Cambridge University Press. 1931.

Lewis F. Day, *Alphabets Old and New.* B. T. Batsford. 1910.

Lewis F. Day, *Penmanship of the XVI, XVII, and XVIII Centuries.* B. T. Batsford, 1911.

Edward F. Strange, *Alphabets, A Manual of Lettering.* G. Bell, 1921.

Peter Jessen, *Meister der Schreibkunst aus drei Jahrhunderten.* Julius Hoffman, Stuttgart. 1923.

Vicentino. Facsimiles of Arrighi's Writing Books, with an introduction by Stanley Morison. Privately printed, Paris. 1926.

Three Classics of Italian Calligraphy. Facsimiles of Writing Books of Arrighi, Tagliente, and Palatino, with an introduction by Oscar Ogg. Dover Publications, New York. 1953.

John Howard Benson, *The First Writing Book.* An English translation and facsimile text of Arrighi's *La Operina.* Oxford University Press: Yale University Press. 1955.

Ludovico Vicentino. Facsimiles of Arrighi's Writing Books. Tidens Förlag, Stockholm. 1958.

La Operina. Facsimile, with foreword by Ejnar Philip and Danish translation by Bent Rohde. Grafiske Højskole, Copenhagen. 1959.

Juan de Yciar. A facsimile of *Arte Subtilissima* with an introduction by Reynolds Stone and a translation by Evelyn Schuckburgh. Oxford University Press, 1960.

Berthold Wolpe, *A Newe Booke of Copies 1574.* Oxford University Press. 1962.

Opera di Giovanniantonio Tagliente. Facsimile of the 1525 edition, with an introduction by James M. Wells. The Newberry Library, Chicago. 1952.

Wolffgang Fugger's *Handwriting Manual.* 1553. A facsimile, with a foreword by Harry Carter. Oxford University Press. 1960.

E. Casamassima, *Trattati di Scrittura del Cinquecento Italiano.* Edizioni di Polifilo, Milan. 1967.

Ray Nash, *American Writing Masters and Copybooks.* The Colonial Society of Massachusetts. 1959.

English Handwriting. Society for Pure English Tracts, Nos. XXIII

(1926) and XXVIII (1927). Edited by Robert Bridges. Notes by Roger Fry, E. A. Lowe, Alfred Fairbank, and the Editor. Oxford University Press.

M. M. Bridges, *The New Handwriting*. Oxford University Press. 1898.

Edward Johnston, *Writing and Illuminating, and Lettering*. John Hogg. 1906.

Edward Johnston, *Manuscript and Inscription Letters*. With 5 plates by A. E. R. Gill. Pitman. 1909.

Graily Hewitt, *Lettering*. Seeley Service & Co. 1930.

Graily Hewitt, *Handwriting: Everyman's Craft*. Kegan Paul, Trench, Trubner. 1938.

Rudolf Koch, *Das Schreibbüchlein*, Bärenreiter-Verlag, Kassel. 1935 (2nd edn).

George Haupt, *Rudolf Koch der Schreiber*, Insel Verlag, Leipzig. 1936.

Alfred Fairbank, *A Handwriting Manual*. Faber & Faber. 1932 (revised and expanded 1960 and 1975.)

Alfred Fairbank, *The Dryad Writing Cards* (originally issued as *The Barking Writing Cards*.) Dryad Press, Leicester. 1935.

Alfred Fairbank, Charlotte Stone, and Winifred Hooper, Series of nine *Beacon Writing Books*. Ginn. 1959–61.

Marion Richardson, *Writing and Writing Patterns*. University of London Press. 1935.

Lettering of Today. Essays by Anna Simons, Percy J. Smith, and Alfred Fairbank, edited by C. C. Holme. Studio. 1937.

Modern Lettering and Calligraphy. Edited by Rathbone Holme and Kathleen M. Frost. Studio. 1954.

Heather Child, *Calligraphy Today*. Studio Books. 1963.

Lettering Today. Edited by John Brinkley. Studio Vista. 1964.

John Howard Benson and Arthur Graham Carey, *The Elements of Lettering*. McGraw-Hill, New York, 1940.

Alexander Nesbitt, *Lettering: The History and Technique*. Prentice-Hall, New York. 1950.

Ralph Douglas, *Calligraphic Lettering*. Watson-Guptill, New York. 1949. Revised 1967.

Erik Lindegren, *ABC of Lettering and Printing Types*. (Three volumes.) Askim, Sweden. 1964–6.

Paul Standard, *Calligraphy's Flowering, Decay, and Restauration*. The Sylvan Press: The Society of Typographic Arts, Chicago. 1947.

Aubrey West, *Written by Hand*. Allen & Unwin. 1951.

Wilfrid Blunt, *Sweet Roman Hand*. James Barrie. 1952.

Walter Kaech. *Rhythm and Proportion in Lettering*. Otto Walter. Olten, Switzerland. 1956.

Italic Handwriting: Some Examples of Everyday Cursive Hands. Selected by Wilfrid Blunt and Will Carter. Newman Neame. 1954.

The Journals of the Society for Italic Handwriting.

Calligraphy and Palaeography: Essays presented to Alfred Fairbank. Edited by A. S. Osley. Faber & Faber. 1965.

ADDITIONAL BIBLIOGRAPHY

Edward Johnston, *A Book of Sample Scripts.* V. & A. Museum. 1966.

Otto Pächt and J. J. G. Alexander, *Illuminated Manuscripts in the Bodleian Library, Oxford.* Vol. 1, Oxford University Press. 1966.

A. S. Osley, *Mercator.* Faber & Faber. 1969.

J. J. G. Alexander and A. C. de la Mare, *Italian Manuscripts in the Library of Major J. R. Abbey.* Faber & Faber. 1969.

P. D'Ancona and E. Aeschlimann, *The Art of Illumination.* Phaidon. 1969.

The Calligrapher's Handbook. Ed. C. M. Lamb. Faber & Faber. 1969.

Donald M. Anderson, *The Art of Written Forms.* Holt, Rinehart & Winston, New York. 1969.

Alfred Fairbank, *The Story of Handwriting.* Faber & Faber. 1970.

Edward Johnston, *Formal Penmanship & Other Papers.* Edited by Heather Child. Lund Humphries. 1971.

T. A. M. Bishop, *English Caroline Minuscule.* Oxford University Press. 1971.

A. S. Osley, *Luminario.* Miland, Nieuwkoop. 1972.

S. Morison, *Politics and Script.* Edited by Nicolas Barker. Oxford University Press. 1972.

A. C. de la Mare, *The Handwriting of Italian Humanists.* Oxford University Press. 1973.

Alfred Fairbank, *Augustino da Siena.* Merrion Press. 1975.

Michael Harvey, *Lettering Design.* Bodley Head. 1975.

Bruce Barker-Benfield, *The Survival of Ancient Literature.* Bodleian Library, Oxford. 1976.

Charles L. Lehman, *Handwriting Models for Schools.* The Alcuin Press, Portland, Oregon. 1976.

LIST OF PLATES

43

31. Italian Book-hands: Roman and Italic. *c.* 1545.
32. From a Papal Brief to Cardinal Wolsey. 27 August 1519.
33. From a Letter to Cardinal Wolsey from Pasqual Spinula, 7 August 1528.
34. From *Libro nel qual s'insegna a scrivere* by G. B. Palatino. 1540.
35. From *Literarum Latinarum* by Gerard Mercator. Antwerp, 1540.
36. From *Thesaurarium Artis Scriptoriæ* by Caspar Neff. Cologne, 1549.
37. From *Opera nella quale si insegna a scrivere* by Vespasiano Amphiareo. Venice, 1554.
38. A Madrigal written by Michelangelo.
39. A Letter to Charles V signed Titiano Pittore (Titian). 8 December 1545.
40. Inscription by Sir John Cheke.
41. From a Letter written by Roger Ascham. 13 February 1546.
42. From a Letter written by Bartholomew Dodington. 12 May 1590.
43. A Letter written by Queen Elizabeth I (when Princess). 1548.
44. From *Arte Subtilissima* by Juan de Yciar. Saragossa, 1555.
45. From *Arte de escrivir* by Francisco Lucas. Madrid, 1577.
46–48. From *Il perfetto Scrittore* by G. F. Cresci. Venice, 1569.
49–51. From *A Booke Containing Divers Sortes of Hands.* Jean de Beauchesne & John Baildon. London, 1570.
52. From *Lo Scrittor' Utile et brieve Segretario* by G. A. Hercolani. Bologna, 1574.
53. From *Spieghel der Schriftkonste* by Jan van den Velde. Rotterdam, 1605.
54. From *The Writing Schoolemaster or The Anatomy of Faire Writing* by John Davies of Hereford. 1663.
55. From *The Pens Excellencie or the Secretaries Delight* by Martin Billingsley. 1618.
56. From *Les Écritures Financière, et Italienne-Bastarde* by Louis Barbedor. Paris, 1647.
57. From an *Office de la Vierge a Matines.* Writing by Nicolas Jarry. Paris, 1659.
58. From *A Compendium of the Usuall Hands* by Richard Daniel. 1664.
59. From *Magnum in Parvo or the Pen's Perfection* by Edward Cocker. 1672.
60. From *Nuncius Oris: A Round-hand Coppy-book* by Caleb Williams. ?1693.

*

The frontispiece is taken from Giovanantonio Tagliente,
Lo presente libro Insegna . . ., 1531.

PLATES

THIS collection of disciplined scripts is to be thought of as an anthology of calligraphy as much as an indication of the background of English contemporary handwriting. It could also be considered as a study in continuity.

A number of hands of importance to the historian are not represented at all, and some of the copperplate examples have been selected more for historical than artistic reasons. The many examples of the scripts of the fifteenth and sixteenth centuries point to the author's interest in this style, but also to the contemporary revival of the italic hand.

Attributions to Renaissance penmen shown in Plates 21, 23, 24, 26, 30, and 32, and Figure 4, are by the author and though supported by the opinion of others have therefore less than certainty of authenticity.

A drastic reduction in size has occasionally been necessary and this is regretted. No reduction, however, has been made in the scripts shown in Plates 2 to 5, 7, 10, 13, 20, 25, 26, 32, 40, 45, 57, and 67. As this is a small book, the carefully arranged margins, so important to the appearance of manuscripts, have been sacrificed. Plates 2 to 27, 30 to 33, 38 to 43, 70, 72 to 74, 76 and 77, are reproductions of writing – mostly on vellum or parchment. The hands shown in Plates 28, 29, 34 to 37, 44 to 56, 58 to 69, 71, 72, 75, 78 to 80, were intended as exemplars.

Where the reproduction is of printed matter, the original method of printing is indicated as follows: Plates 28, 29, 34 to 37, and 44 to 51, wood-cuts; Plates 52 to 56, and 58 to 67, engraved metal plates; Plate 59, engraved silverplate; Plates 68 and 69, lithography; Plate 71, collotype; Plates 78 and 79, line blocks; and Plate 80, offset-lithography.

B.M. = British Museum   V. and A.M. = Victoria and Albert Museum
P.R.O. = Public Record Office   B.L. = Bodleian Library, Oxford

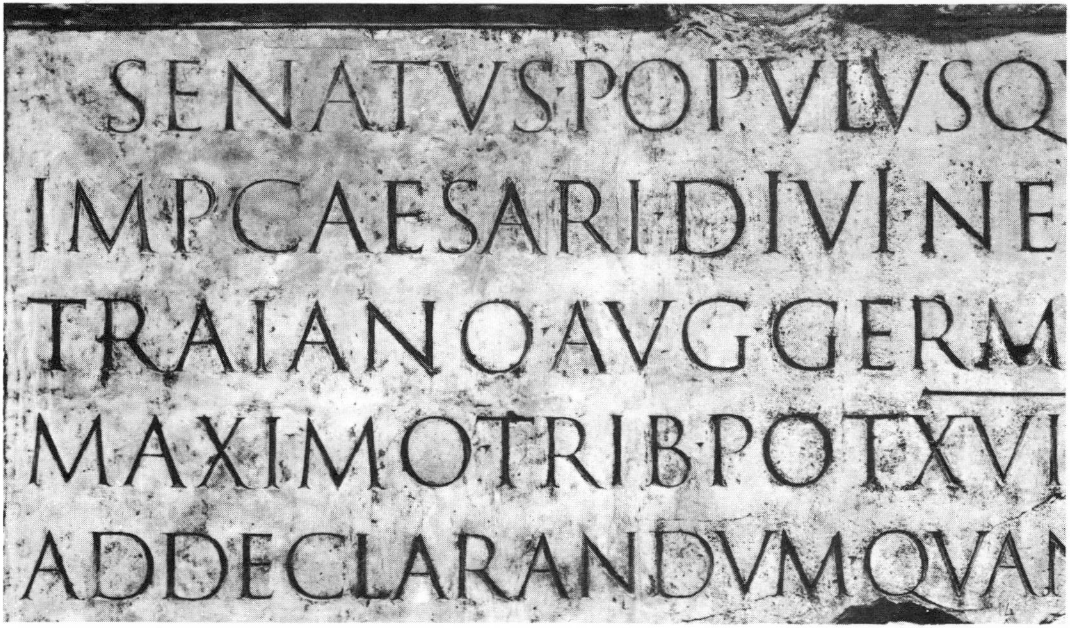

Plate 1. From a plaster cast in the V. and A.M. of an inscription cut in stone on the base of the Trajan Column in Rome. A.D.114.

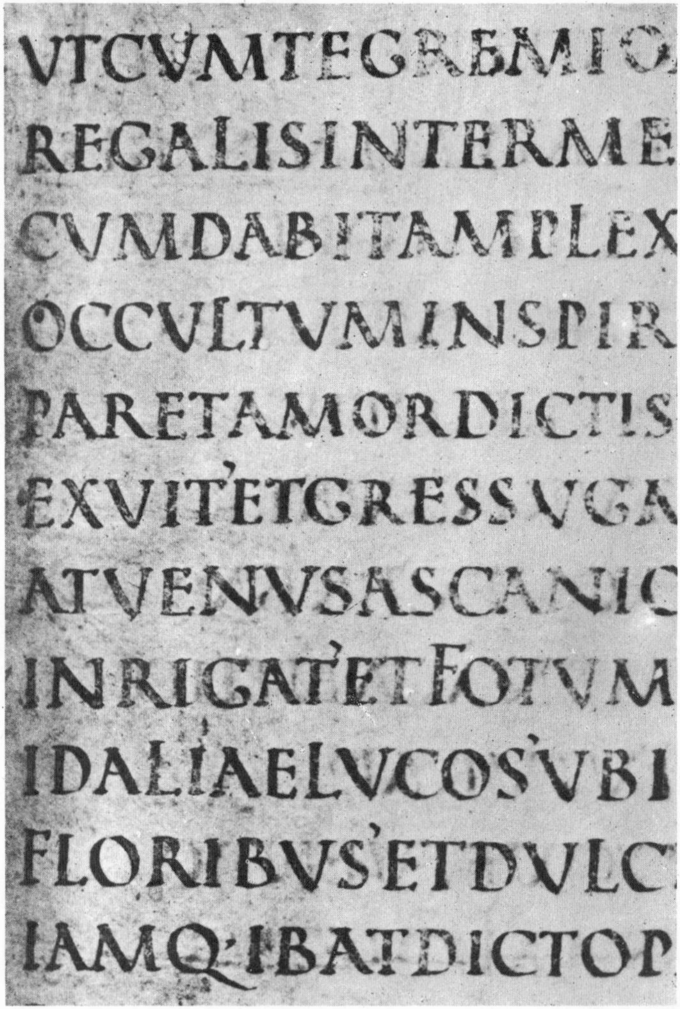

VTCVMTEGREMIO
REGALISINTERME
CVMDABITAMPLEX
OCCVLTVMINSPIR
PARETAMORDICTIS
EXVITETGRESSVGA
ATVENVSASCANIO
INRIGATETFOTVM
IDALIAELVCOSVBI
FLORIBVSETDVLC
IAMQ·IBATDICTOP

Plate 2. From a Virgil in the Library of St Gall (Cod. 1394). Square Capitals.
4th or 5th century.

SCALAEIMPROVISOSUBIT
DISCVRRVNTALIIADPORT
FERRVMALIITORQVENTE
IPSEINTERPRIMOSDEXTR
AENEASMAGNAQVEINCI
TESTATVRQVEDEOSITERVM
BISIAMITALOSHOSTISTEN
EXORITVRTREPIDOSINTE
VRBEMALIIRESARAREIV
DARDANIDISIPSVMQVET
ARMATERVNIAIFTPERGV
INCIVSASVTCVMLATEBR
VESTIGAVITAPESETFVMO
ILLAEINTVSTREPIDAERER
DISCVRRVNTMAGNISQVE

Plate 3. From a Virgil in the Vatican Library (Cod. Palat. Lat. 1631). Rustic Capitals. Perhaps of the 4th–5th century.

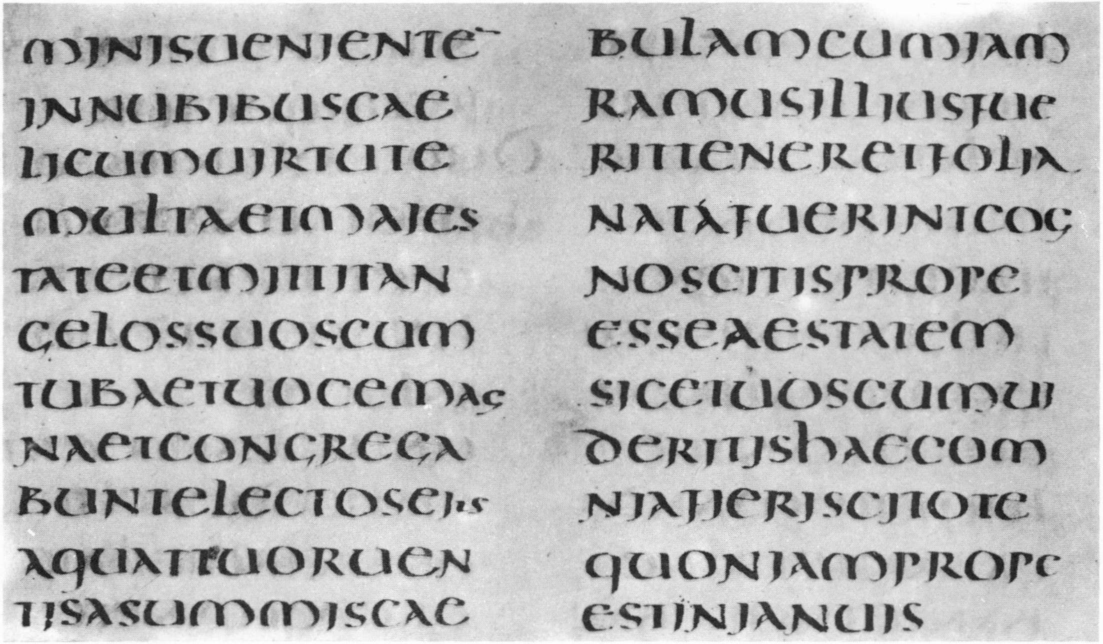

Plate 4. From *Evangeliario*. Uncials. 5th century. France. Biblioteca Vaticana (Vat. Lat. 7223, f. 50r).

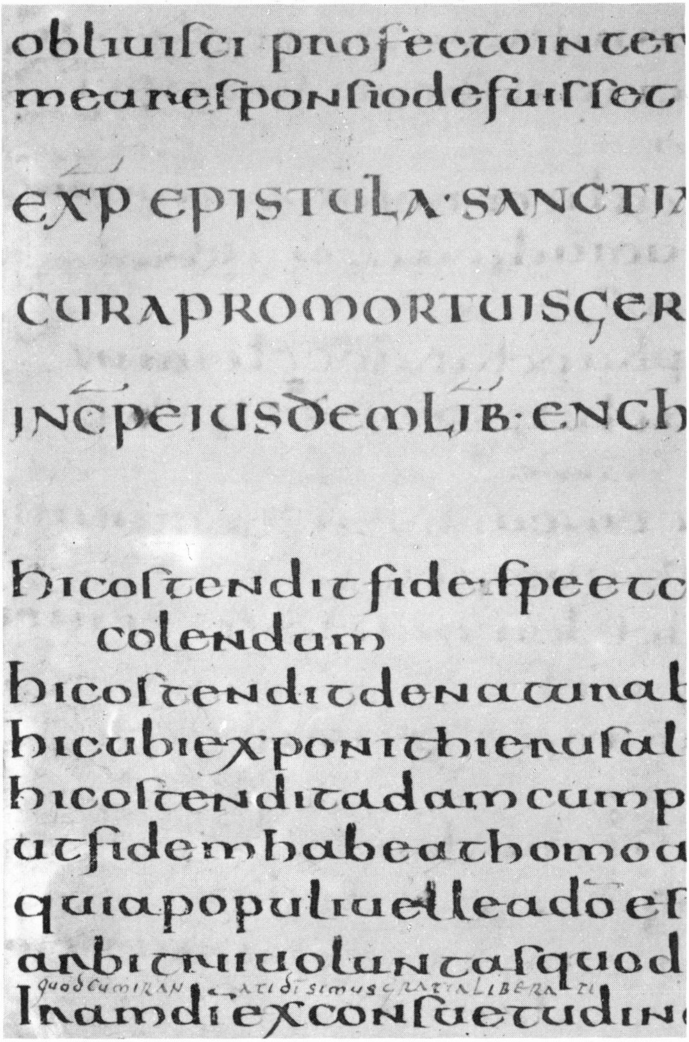

obliuifci profectointer
mea refponfiodefuiffec

exp epistula·sancti/

curapromortuisçer

incpeiusoemljb·ench

hicoftendit fide·fpeetc
coleNdum
hicoftendictdenacunal
hicubiexponichierufal
hicoftenditadamcump
utfidemhabeathomou
quiapopuliuelleadoef
anbitruiuoluncafquod
quodeumiran ftiofsimuscrattaliberati
Inamdiexconfuetudin

Plate 5. From *Works of St Jerome and St Augustine.* Uncials and Half-uncials.
6th century. S. Italy. Bamberg (B.IV.21).

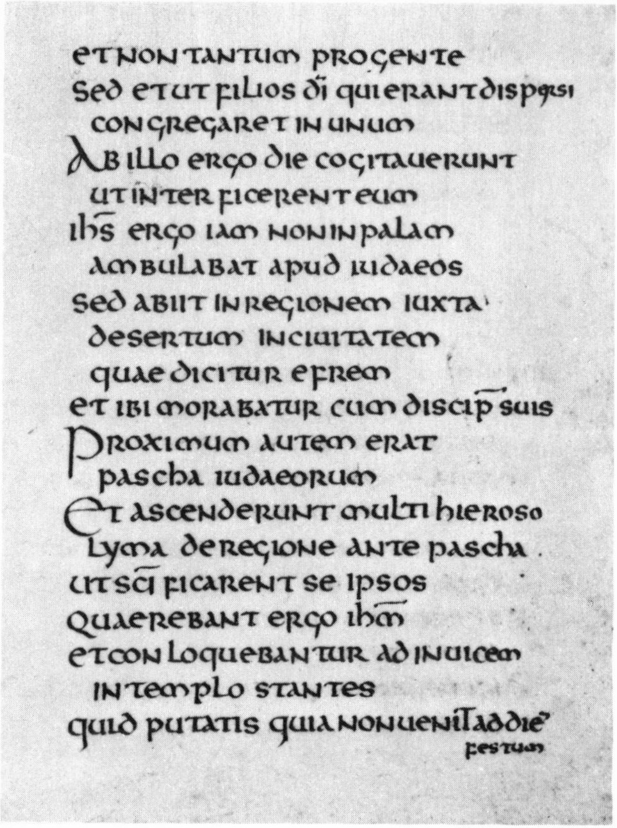

ETNON TANTUM PROGENTE
SED ETUT FILIOS DI QUI ERANTDISPGSI
CONGREGARET IN UNUM
AB ILLO ERGO DIE COGITAUERUNT
UT INTER FICERENT EUM
IHS ERGO IAM NON IN PALAM
AMBULABAT APUD IUDAEOS
SED ABIIT IN REGIONEM IUXTA
DESERTUM IN CIUITATEM
QUAE DICITUR EFREM
ET IBI MORABATUR CUM DISCIP SUIS
PROXIMUM AUTEM ERAT
PASCHA IUDAEORUM
ET ASCENDERUNT MULTI HIEROSO
LYMA DE REGIONE ANTE PASCHA
UT SCI FICARENT SE IPSOS
QUAEREBANT ERGO IHM
ETCON LOQUEBANTUR AD INUICEM
IN TEMPLO STANTES
QUID PUTATIS QUIA NON UENIT AD DIE
                                    FESTUM

Plate 6. From *The Gospel of St John*. Uncials. Probably written at Jarrow or Wearmouth in the 7th century. Found in the tomb of St Cuthbert (d. 678) in 1104. Library of Stonyhurst College.

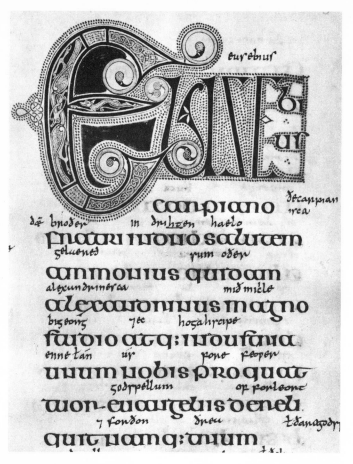

Plate 7. From the *Lindisfarne Gospels.* Written in insular half-uncials, before A.D. 698 by Eadfrith, Bishop of Lindisfarne, in honour of St Cuthbert. The Anglo-Saxon translation was added between the lines by the priest Aldred in the 10th century. B.M. (Cotton MS. Nero D.iv). A modernized version of this hand was shown by Edward Johnston in *Writing and Illuminating, and Lettering.*

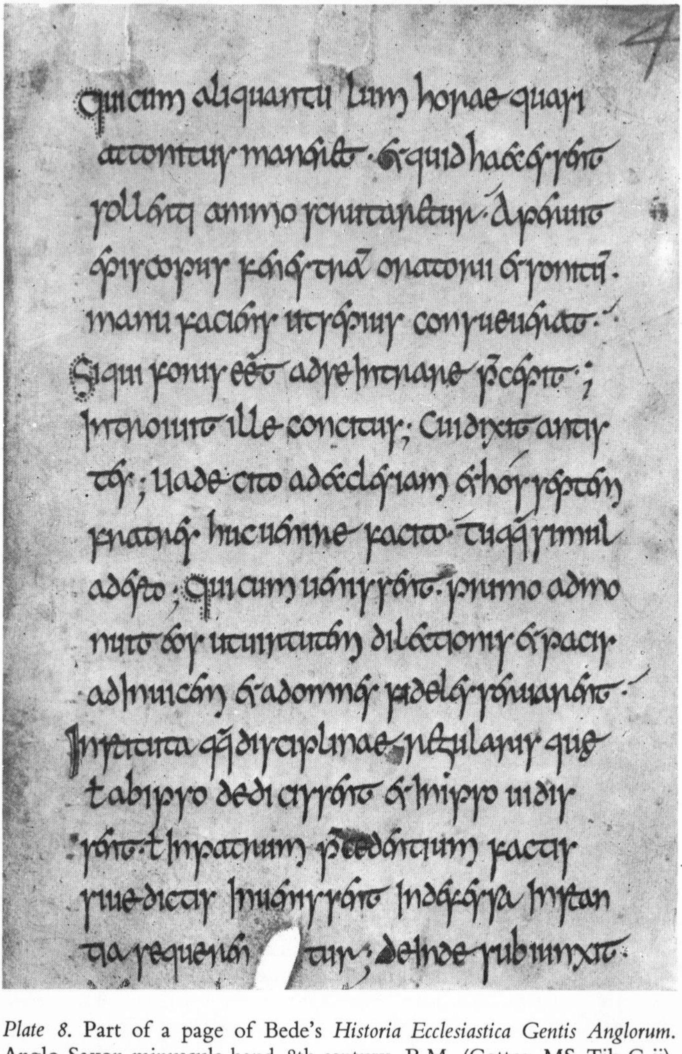

Plate 8. Part of a page of Bede's *Historia Ecclesiastica Gentis Anglorum.*
Anglo-Saxon minuscule hand. 8th century. B.M. (Cotton MS. Tib. C. ii).

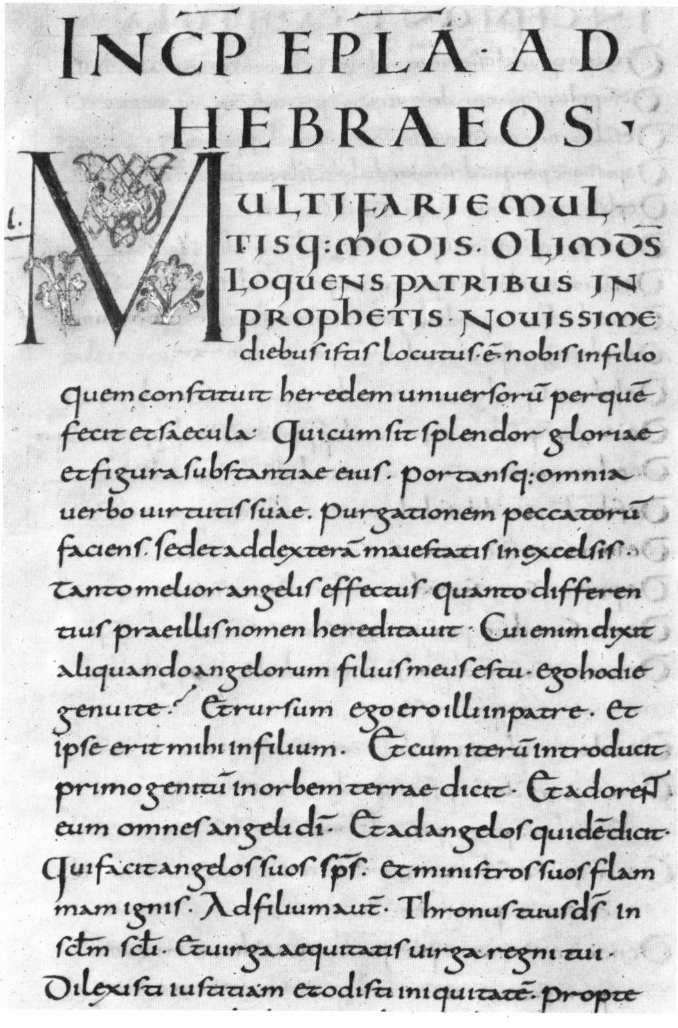

INCP EPLA AD
HEBRAEOS ·

Multifarie mul
tisq: modis olim ds
loquens patribus in
prophetis Nouissime
diebus istis locutus e nobis infilio
quem constituit heredem uniuersoru perque
fecit et saecula Quicum sit splendor gloriae
et figura substantiae eius. portansq: omnia
uerbo uirtutis suae. purgationem peccatoru
faciens. sedet ad dexteram maiestatis inexcelsis
tanto melior angelis effectus quanto differen
tius prae illis nomen hereditauit · Cui enim dixit
aliquando angelorum filius meus es tu egohodie
genuite.' Et rursum ego ero illi in patre. Et
ipse erit mihi infilium. Et cum iteru introducit
primogenitu in orbem terrae dicit. Et adorent
eum omnes angeli di. Et ad angelos quide dicit
Qui facit angelos suos sps. Et ministros suos flam
mam ignis. Ad filium aut. Thronus tuus ds in
sctm scti. Et uirga aequitatis uirga regni tui ·
Dilexisti iustitiam et odisti iniquitate propte

Plate 9. From a Bible in the Latin Vulgate version as revised by Alcuin of York. Roman capitals, uncials, and Caroline minuscules. Written at Tours about the middle of the 9th century B.M. (Add. MS. 10546).

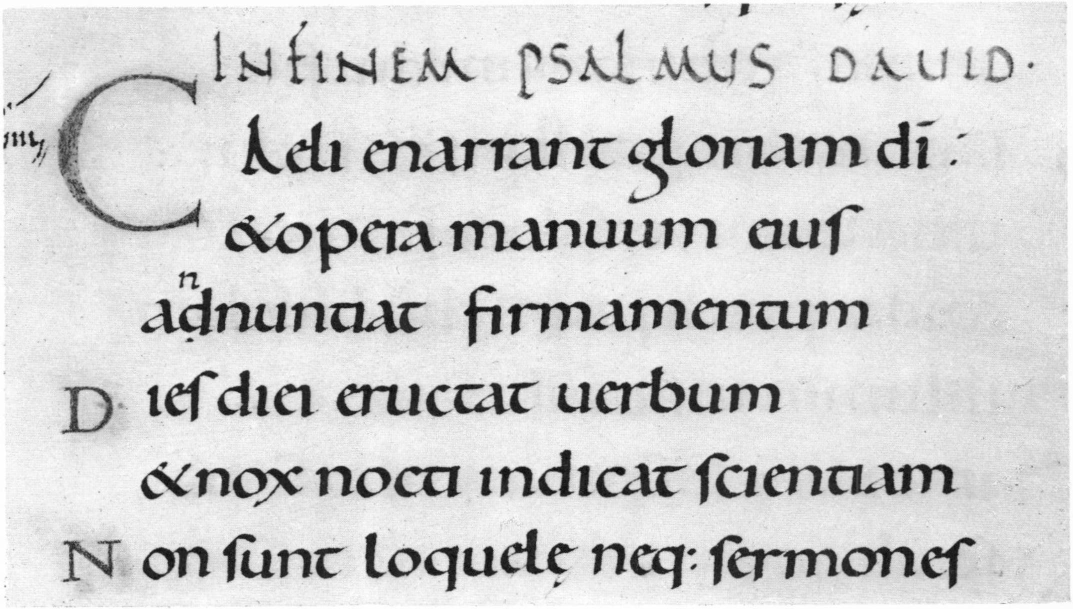

INFINEM PSALMUS DAUID·
CAELI ENARRANT GLORIAM DĪ·
& OPERA MANUUM EIUS
ADNUNTIAT FIRMAMENTUM
DIES DIEI ERUCTAT UERBUM
& NOX NOCTI INDICAT SCIENTIAM
NON SUNT LOQUELE NEQ: SERMONES

Plate 10. From a Psalter written in southern England about A.D. 975. B.M. (Harl. MS. 2904). Edward Johnston regarded this script as 'an almost perfect model for a formal hand' and he taught a modernized version which he called 'The Foundational Hand' (cf. *Plate 72*).

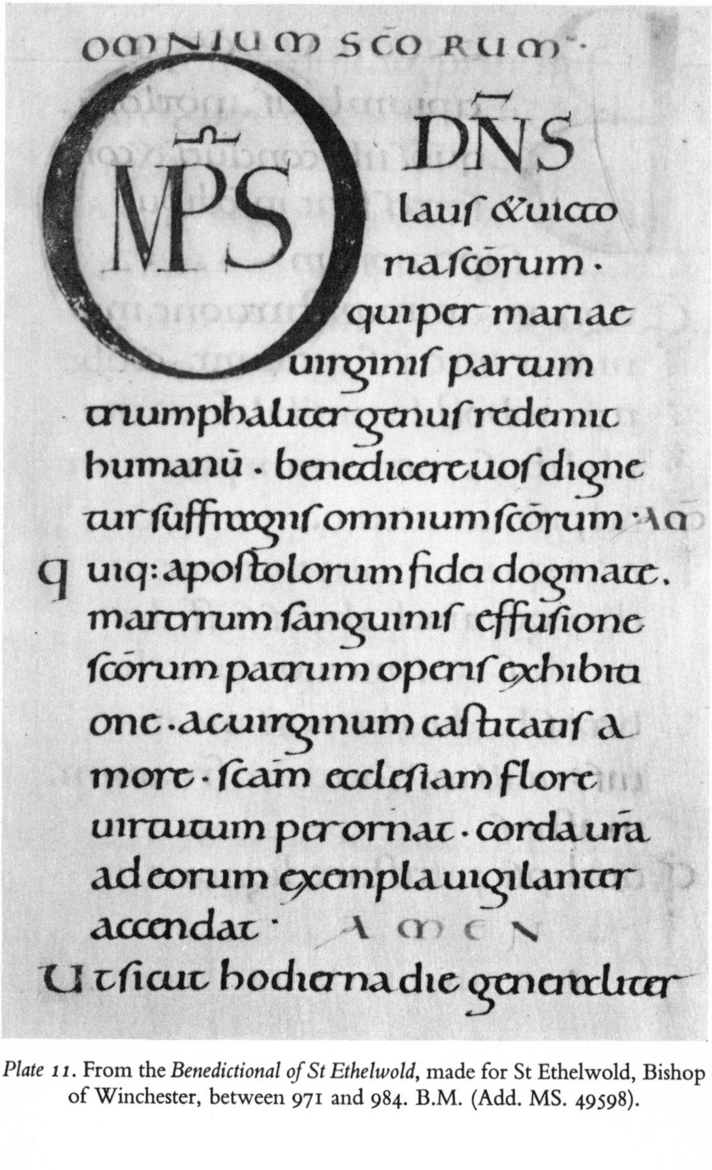

DNS
lauſ & uicto
ria ſcōrum ·
qui per mariae
uirginiſ partum
triumphaliter genuſ redemit
humanū · benedicere uoſ digne
tur ſuffragiiſ omnium ſcōrum · A
q uiq: apoſtolorum fida dogmate ·
martyrum ſanguiniſ effuſione
ſcōrum patrum operiſ exhibiti
one · ac uirginum caſtitatiſ a
more · ſcam eccleſiam flore
uirtutum perornat · corda uſa
ad eorum exempla uigilanter
accendat · AMEN
Ut ſiciat hodierna die generaliter

Plate 11. From the *Benedictional of St Ethelwold*, made for St Ethelwold, Bishop of Winchester, between 971 and 984. B.M. (Add. MS. 49598).

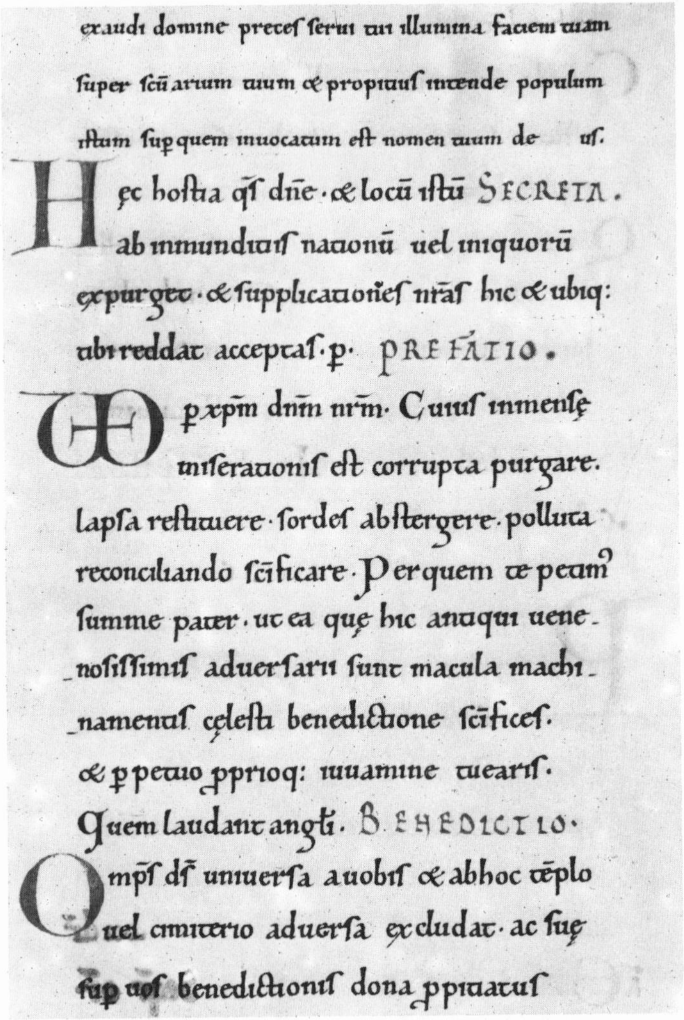

exaudi domine preces serui tui illumina faciem tuam

super scuarium tuum & propitius intende populum

istum sup quem inuocatum est nomen tuum de   us.

Hęc hostia qs dñe · & locū istū SECRETA.

ab immundiciis nationū uel iniquorū

expurget · & supplicationes ntas hic & ubiq:

ubi reddat acceptas · p· PREFATIO.

p xpm dñm nrm. Cuius inmensę

miserationis est corrupta purgare.

lapsa restituere · sordes abstergere · polluta

reconciliando scificare · Per quem te petm̃

summe pater · ut ea quę hic antiqui uene_

nosissimis aduersarii sunt macula machi

_namentis cęlesti benedictione scifices.

& ppetio pprioq: iuuamine tuearis.

Quem laudant angli. BENEDICTIO.

Omps dñs uniuersa a uobis & ab hoc templo

uel cimiterio aduersa excludat · ac suę

sup uos benedictionis dona ppitiatus

Plate 12. From a Benedictional. 11th century. B.M. (Add. MS. 28188).
Written in black, red, blue and green inks.

ad Spalduic manerium abbis de Ely. 7 sic abb ha
buit. T.R.E. 7 post aduent W. regis V. annis.
hanc Eustachi' ui de eccla rapuit 7 retinuit.
/ Kerelestan dnm fuisse 7 ee. de firma regis ESW.
7 quamis Aluric' uicecomes sedisset in ea uilla tam
sep reddebat de ea firma regis 7 filii ei' post eu.
donec Eustachi' accepit uicecomitatu. nec unqua
uide' uel audier sigillu regis.E. qd ea forismisisset
de firma sua.
/ Aluuot s' 7 frs clamant Eustachiu sibi iniuste tra
sua abstulisse. 7 comitat' negat se uidisse sigillu
uel saisitore qui eu inde saisisset.
/ La die quaijex.E. fuit uiuus 7 mortuus. fuit Gece
linge Berewic' in Almundeberie. in firma regis.
/ Comitat' testificat' Buchestutiorde fuisse Berewich
in pachstone. T.R.E.
/ Triginta vi acre in brauuine quas Ricard clamat
ad foresta pertinere. dnt de dnica firma regis fuisse.
nec ad foresta pertinuisse.
/ Grasha dnt soca regis fuisse 7 esse. nec breue nec
saisitore uidisse qui liber. istit ea Eustachio.
/ De .vi. hidis in Connetune dirent se audisse

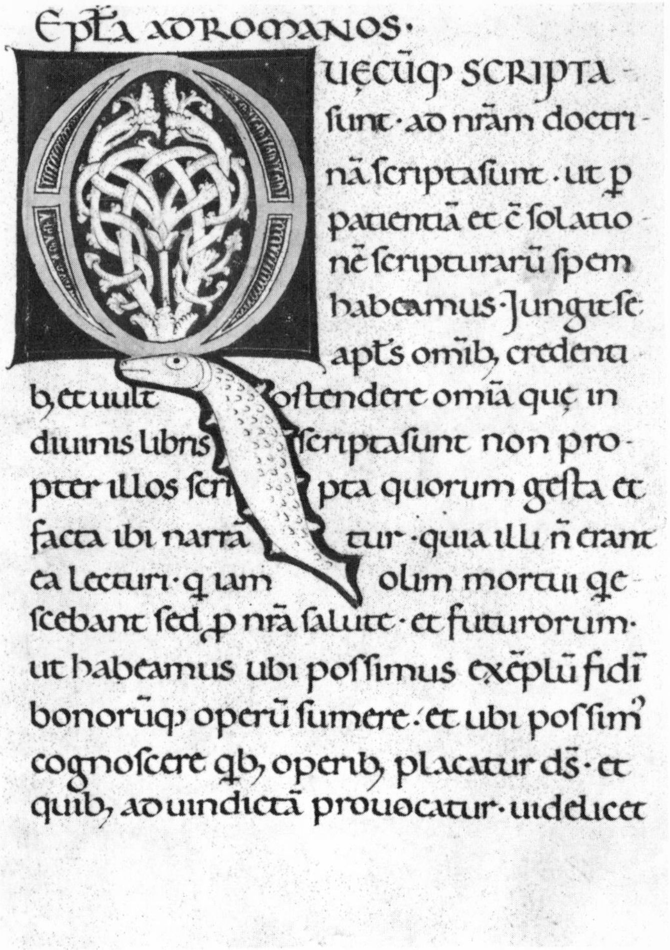

ЄPꞮ̄A AD ROMANOS·

UECŨQ SCRIPTA
sunt · ad nr̄am doctri-
nā scriptasunt · ut p
patientiā et c̄ solatio-
nē scripturarū spem
habeamus· Jungit se:
apt's omib, credenti
b, et uult ostendere omīa quç in
diuinis libris scriptasunt non pro-
pter illos scri pta quorum gesta et
facta ibi narrā tur · quia illi ñ erant
ea lecturi · q̄ iam olim mortui ge-
scebant sed, p nr̄ā salute · et futurorum·
ut habeamus ubi possimus exēplū fidi
bonorūq operū sumere · et ubi possim'
cognoscere qb, operib, placatur dš· et
quib, ad uindictā prouocatur· uidelicet

Plate 14. From an Italian MS. of Homilies and Lessons. First part of 12th century. B.M. (Harl. MS. 7183).

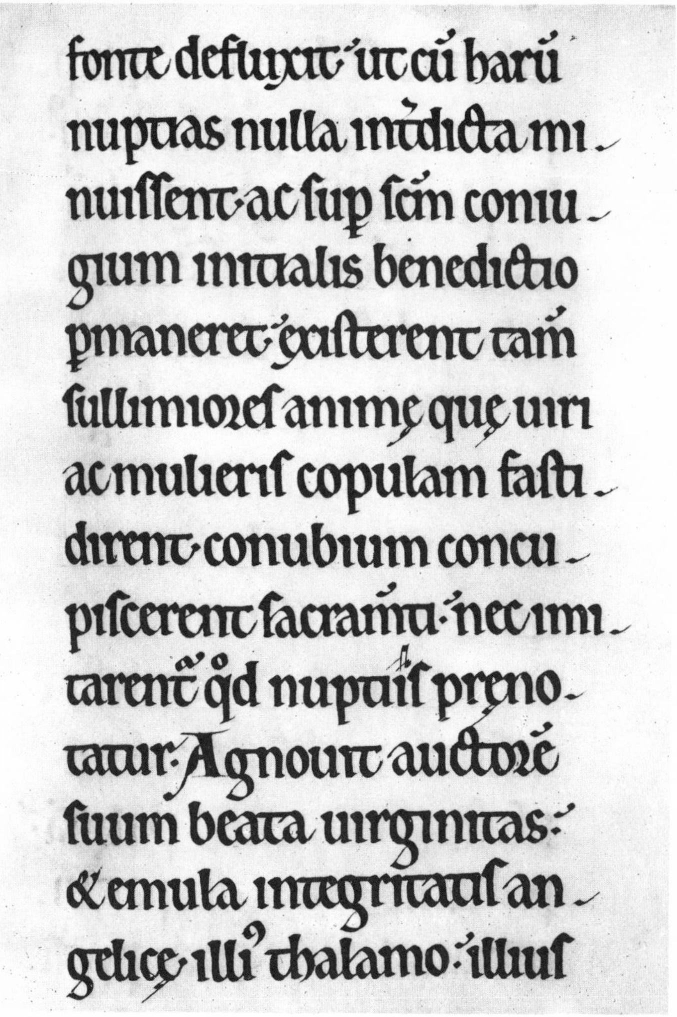

fonte defluxit · ut cũ harũ
nuptias nulla intdicta mi
nuissent · ac sup scm coniu
gium initialis benedictio
pmaneret · existerent tam
sullimiores animę quę uiri
ac mulieris copulam fasti
dirent · conubium concu
piscerent sacramtu · nec imi
tarent qd nuptiis pręno
tatur · Agnouit auctorę
suum beata uirginitas ·
& emula integritatis an
gelicę · illi° thalamo · illius

Plate 15. From a Pontifical. English writing of 12th century.
B.M. (Cotton MS. Tib. B. viii).

Plate 16. Gothic script of a French Prayer-book. *c.*1386. B.L. (MS. Rawl. liturg. e. 40, 15829). From *Florilegium Alphabeticum* by B. L. Wolpe in *Calligraphy and Palaeography*.

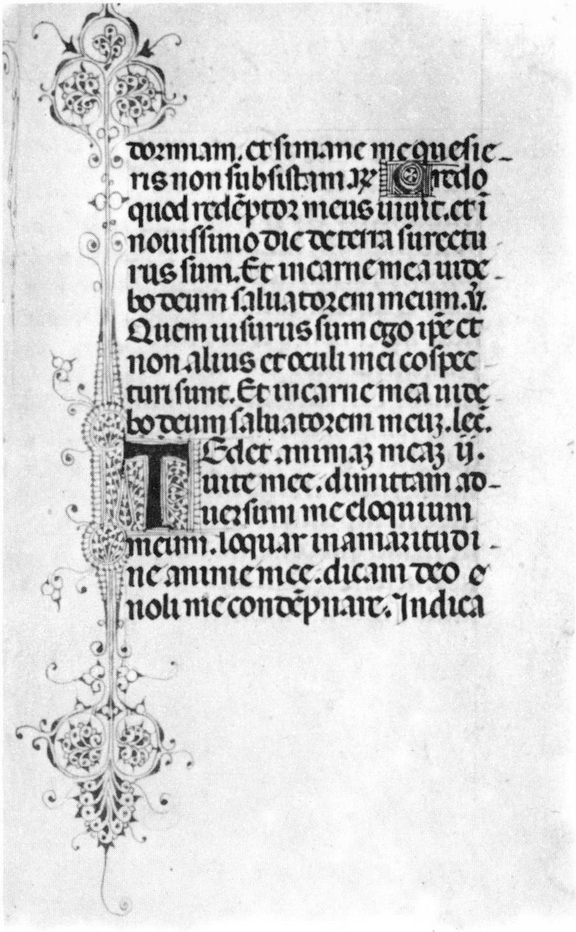

Plate 17. Littera rotunda script from a Book of Hours.
Written in Italy in the late 14th century. B.M. (Add. MS. 34247).

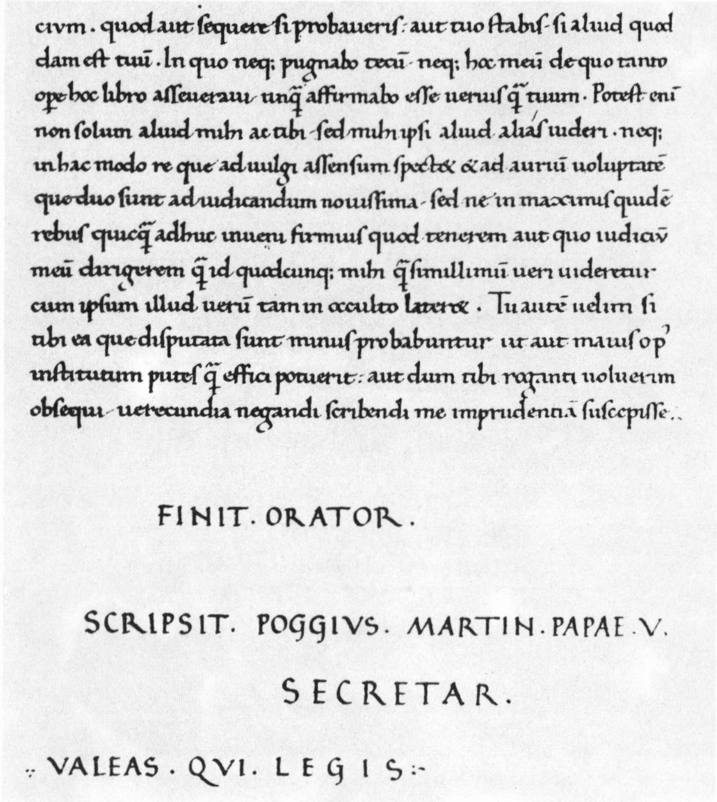

cium. quod aut sequere si probaueris: aut tuo stabis si aliud quod
dam est tuu. In quo neq; pugnabo tecu neq; hoc meu de quo tanto
ope hoc libro asseuerani unq affirmabo esse uerius q̃ tuum. Potest eni
non solum aliud mihi ac tibi sed mihi ipsi aliud alias uideri. neq;
in hac modo re que ad uulgi assensum spectat & ad auriu uoluptate
que duo sunt ad iudicandum nouissima sed ne in maximis quide
rebus quicq̃ adhuc inueni firmius quod tenerem aut quo iudicui
meu dirigerem q̃ id quodcunq; mihi q̃ simillimu ueri uideretur
cum ipsum illud ueru tam in occulto lateret. Tu aute uelim si
tibi ea que disputata sunt minus probabuntur ut aut maius op
institutum putes q̃ effici potuerit: aut dum tibi roganti noluerim
obsequi uerecundia negandi scribendi me imprudentia suscepisse.

FINIT. ORATOR.

SCRIPSIT. POGGIVS. MARTIN. PAPAE. V.

SECRETAR.

VALEAS. QVI. LEGIS.

Plate 18. From *Cicero: De Oratore*. Written by Poggio Bracciolini. 1425.
Bibl. Laur., Florence (Plut. 59. 31). (From *Renaissance Handwriting*.)

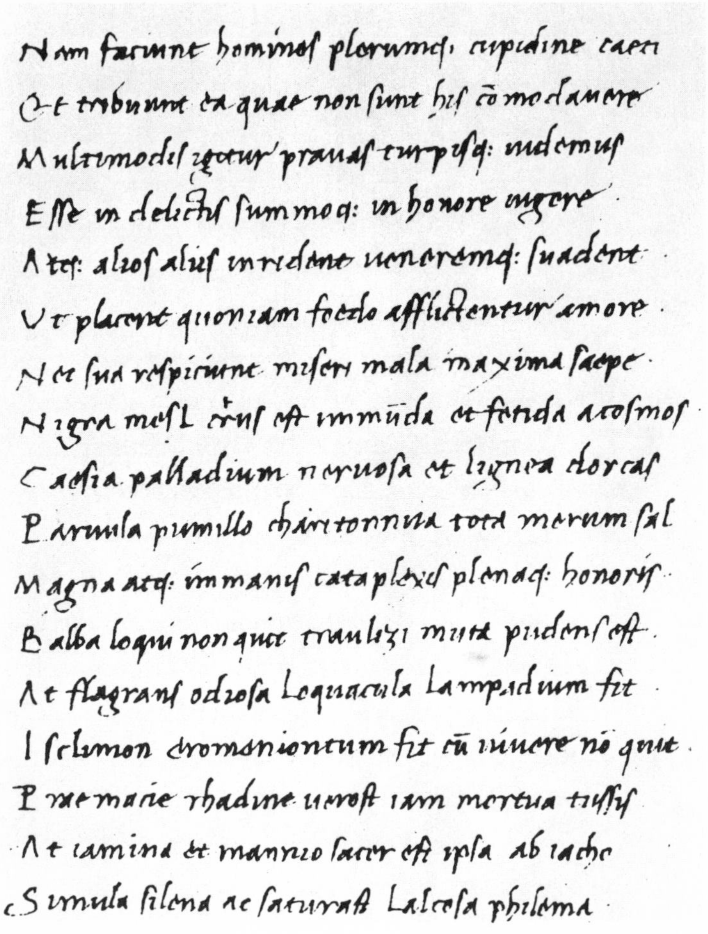

Nam faciunt homines plerumq; cupidine caeci
Et tribuunt ea quae non sunt his comoda uere
Multimodis igitur prauas turpisq; uidemus
Esse in deliciis summoq; in honore uigere
Atq; alios alii inrident ueneremq; suadent
Vt placent quoniam foedo afflictentur amore
Nec sua respiciunt miseri mala maxima saepe
Nigra melſ crus est immuda et fetida acosmos
Caesia palladium neruosa et lignea dorcas
Paruula pumillo chariton mia tota merum sal
Magna atq; immanes cataplexis plenaq; honoris
Balba loqui non quit traulizi muta pudens est
At flagrans odiosa loquacula lampadium fit
Ischnon eromenion tum fit cum uiuere no quit
Prae macie rhadine uerost iam mortua tussis
At tumida et mammoso cerer est ipsa ab iaccho
Simula silena ac saturast labeosa philema

Plate 19. From *Lucretius.* Written by Niccolo Niccoli. 1423(?).
Bibl. Laur., Florence (Laur. 35.30).

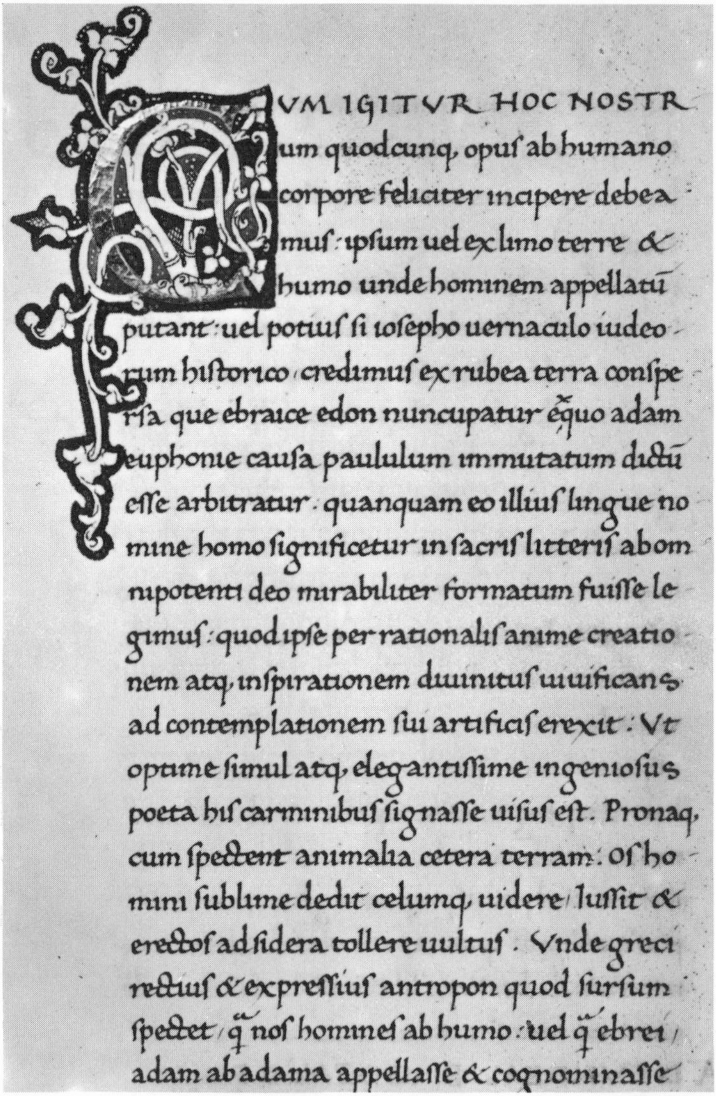

VM IGITVR HOC NOSTR
um quodcunq, opus ab humano
corpore feliciter incipere debea
mus ipsum uel ex limo terre &
humo unde hominem appellatu
putant uel potius si iosepho uernaculo iudeo
rum historico credimus ex rubea terra conspe
rsa que ebraice edon nuncupatur eq̃uo adam
euphonie causa paululum immutatum dictu
esse arbitratur quanquam eo illius lingue no
mine homo significetur in sacris litteris ab om
nipotenti deo mirabiliter formatum fuisse le
gimus quod ipse per rationalis anime creatio
nem atq, inspirationem diuinitus uiuificans
ad contemplationem sui artificis erexit Vt
optime simul atq, elegantissime ingeniosus
poeta his carminibus signasse uisus est. Pronaq,
cum spectent animalia cetera terram os ho
mini sublime dedit celumq, uidere iussit &
erectos ad sidera tollere uultus Vnde greci
rectius & expressius antropon quod sursum
spectet q̃ nos homines ab humo uel q̃ ebrei
adam ab adama appellasse & cognominasse

Plate 20. From *De Dignitate et Excellentia Hominis.* Written in humanistic script by Gherardo del Ciriagio at Florence. 1454. B.M. (Harl. MS. 2593, f.3 v.)

Mortuus inferna uulnera lauit aqua:

Cynthia quin etiam uersu laudata opperti

Hos inter si me ponere fama uolet;

LIBER TERTIVS

ALLIMACHI manes: & coi

sacra philetæ

In uestrum quæso me sinite

ire nemus:

Primus ego ingredior puro

de fonte sacerdos

Itala per graios orgia ferre choros

Dicite quo pariter carmen tenuistis in antro:

Quo ue pede ingressi: qua ue bibistis aquam

Ah ualeat phœbum quicunq; moratur in armis

Exactus tenui pumice uersus eat:

Quo me fama leuat terra sublimis: & a me

Nata coronatis musa triumphat equis:

Et mecum in curru parui uectant amores

Scriptorumq; meas turba secuta rotas:

Quid frustra missis in me certatis habenis:

Non datur ad musas currere lata uia:

Multi Roma tuas laudes annalibus addent

Qui finem imperii bactra futura canent:

Plate 21. From *Propertius: Elegies.* Writing attributed to Antonio Sinibaldi. *c.*1480. B.L. (MS. Canon. class. lat. 31).

quem emulari studiis cupio. Sed utinam ut sa
cerdotium idem ut consulatum multo etiam iu-
uenior q̄ ille sum consecutus. Ita senex saltem
ingenium eius aliqua ex parte assequi possim. S3
nimirum quae sunt in manu hominum & mihi
& multis contingerunt. Illud uero ut adipisci ar-
duum: sic etiam sperare nimium est.´ quod dari
nisi ad iis non potest. vale.

C. plinius vrso suo salutem. Lxxiiii.
Ausam per hos dies dixit iulius bassus homo
laboriosus & aduersis suis clarus. Accusatus ē
sub uespasiano a duobus priuatis ad senatum
remissus diu pependit. tandem absolutus uindi-
catus q̄ est. Titum timuit ut domitiani amicus.
a domitiano relegatus est reuocatus a nerua. so-
titus q̄ bithiniam. Redit reus accusatus non minus acriter q̄ fideliter defensus. uarias sententi-
as habuit. plures tamen mitiores. Egit contra
eum pomponius rufus uir peritus & uehemens.
Rufo successit theophanes, unus ex legatis: fax
accusationis & origo. Respondi ego tiam mihi bassus iniunxerat ut totius defensionis fundamen-
ta iacerem. dicerem de ornamentis suis: quae illi
ex generis claritate & ex periculis ipsis magna erat.
Dicerem de conspiratione delatorum: quam in ques-
tu habebant. dicerem causas quibus factiosissimum

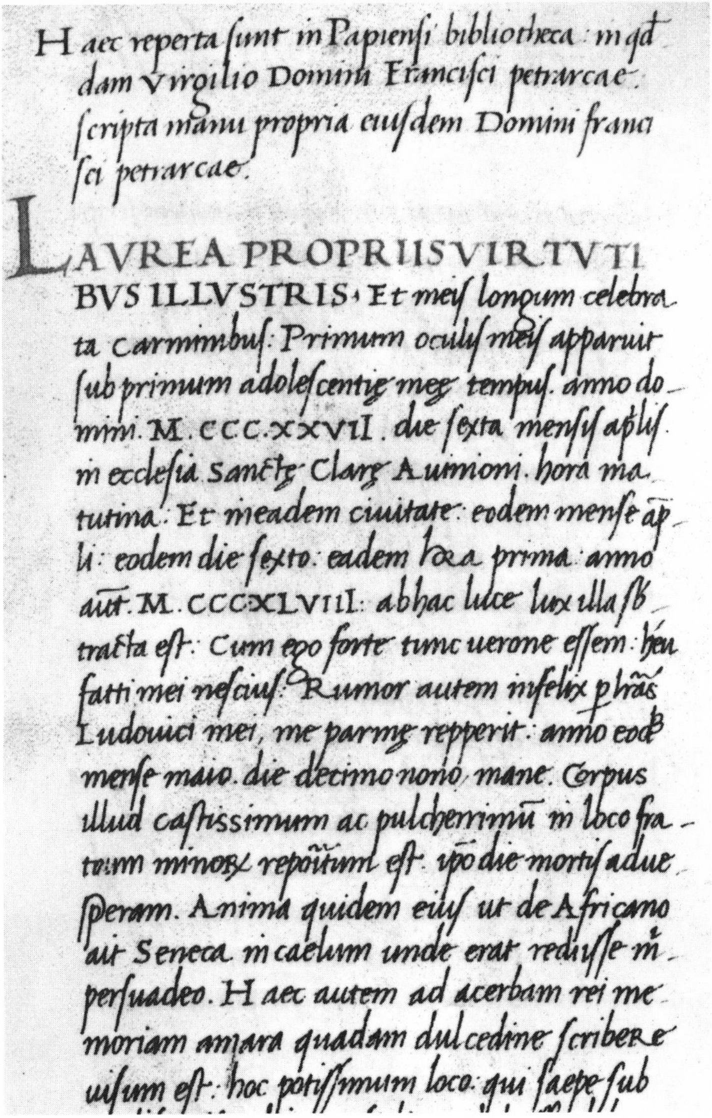

Haec reperta sunt in Papiensi bibliotheca, in qd
dam Virgilio Domini Francisci petrarcae
scripta manu propria eiusdem Domini franci
sci petrarcae.

LAVREA PROPRIIS VIRTVTI
BVS ILLVSTRIS. Et meis longum celebra
ta carminibus. Primum oculis meis apparuit
sub primum adolescentie mee tempus. anno do
mini. M.CCC.XXVII. die sexta mensis aplis.
in ecclesia sancte Clare Auinioni. hora ma
tutina. Et in eadem ciuitate. eodem mense ap
li. eodem die sexto. eadem hora prima. anno
aut. M.CCCXLVIII. abhac luce lux illa sb
tracta est. Cum ego forte tunc uerone essem. heu
fatti mei nescius. Rumor autem infelix p hras
Ludouici mei, me parme repperit. anno eod
mense maio. die decimo nono. mane. Corpus
illud castissimum ac pulcherrimu in loco fra
trum minorz repositum est. ipso die mortis adue
speram. Anima quidem eius ut de Africano
ait Seneca. in caelum unde erat rediisse in
persuadeo. Haec autem ad acerbam rei me
moriam amara quadam dulcedine scribere
uisum est. hoc potissimum loco. qui saepe sub

Plate 23. From *Petrarch: Sonnets*, etc. Writing attributed to Antonio Tophio.
Fitzwilliam Museum, Cambridge (MS. J.170).

P·OVIDII NASO
NIS DE REMEDO
AMORIS LIB·I·

LEGERAT
huius amor nomen
titulumq̄: libelli:
Bella mihi uideo:
bella parantur ait·
Parce tuū uate ſcele
ris damnare cupido

Tradita qui totiens: te duce: ſigna tuli·

Non ego tydides a quo tua ſaucia mater
  In liquidum rediit æquora martis equis·

Sæpe tepent alii iuuenes: ego ſemp amaui:
  Et ſiquid faciam: nunc quoq̄: quæris amo·

Quin& docui qua poſſes arte parari:
  Et q̄d nunc ratio eſt: impetus ante fuit·

Nec te blande puer: nec noſtras prodimus artes:
  Nec noua præteritum muſa retexit opus·

Siquis amat q̄d amare iuuat: feliciter ard&:
  Gaudeat: & uento nauig& ille ſuo·

At ſiquis male fert indignæ regna puellæ:
  Ne pereat: noſtræ ſentiat artis opem·

Plate 24. P.Ovid: Remedia Amoris. Writing attributed to Bartolomeo San Vito.
Bibliothèque Nationale, Paris (Latin 7997, f.180r).

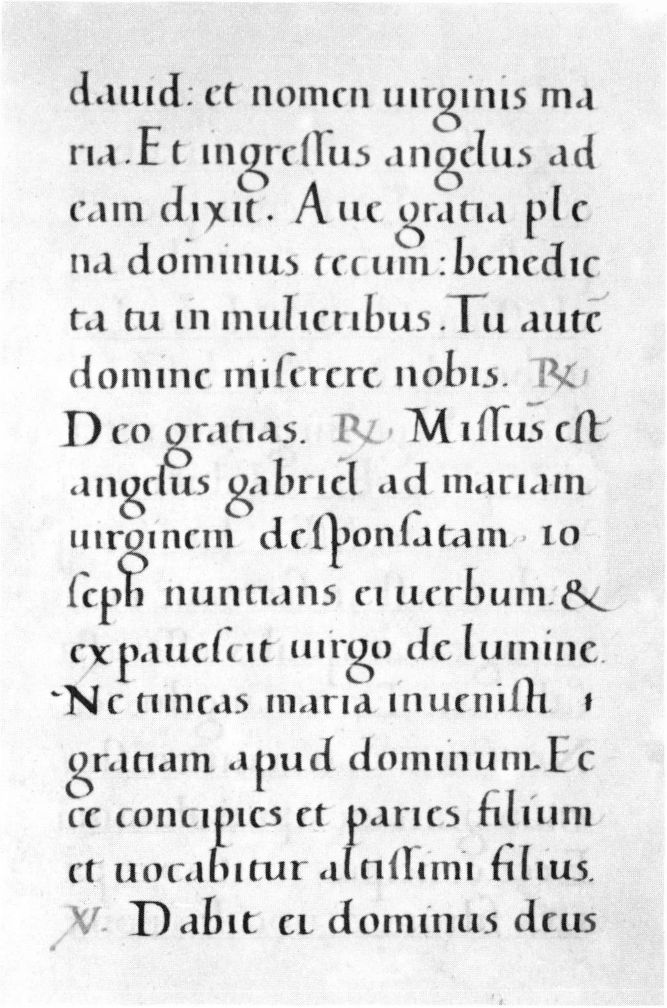

dauid: et nomen uirginis ma
ria. Et ingreſſus angelus ad
eam dixit. Aue gratia ple
na dominus tecum: benedic
ta tu in mulieribus. Tu autē
domine miſerere nobis. ℞
Deo gratias. ℞ Miſſus eſt
angelus gabriel ad mariam
uirginem deſponſatam io
ſeph nuntians ei uerbum. &
expaueſcit uirgo de lumine.
Ne timeas maria inueniſti
gratiam apud dominum. Ec
ce concipies et paries filium
et uocabitur altiſſimi filius.
℣. Dabit ei dominus deus

Plate 25. From the *Hours of Bonaparte Ghislieri of Bologna*. Writing attributed
to Pierantonio Sallando. 1500. B.M. (Yates Thompson MS. 29).

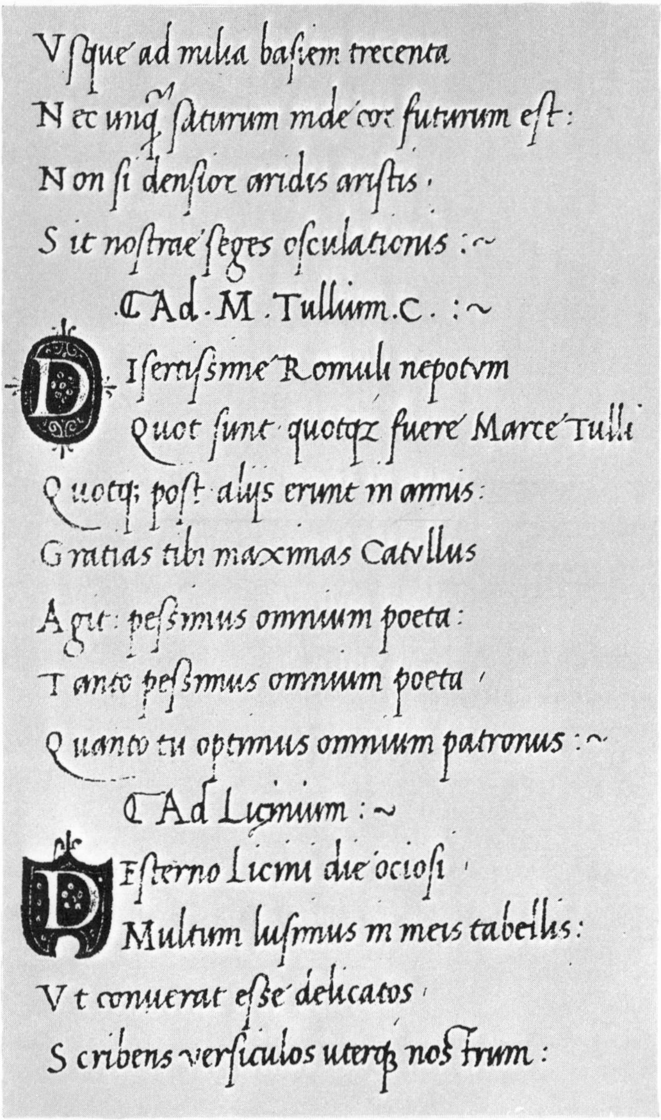

Vsque ad milia basiem trecenta
Nec uniq̃ saturum mde cor futurum est:
Non si densior aridis aristis.
Sit nostrae seges osculationis :~

      ℃ Ad . M . Tullium . C . :~

Disertissime Romuli nepotvm
     Quot sunt quotq̃ fuere Marce Tulli
Quotq̃; post alijs erunt in annis:
Gratias tibi maximas Catvllus
Agit: pessimus omnium poeta:
Tanto pessimus omnium poeta
Quanto tu optimus omnium patronus :~

      ℃ Ad Licinium :~

Esterno Licini die ociosi
     Multum lusimus in meis tabellis:
Vt conuerat esse delicatos
Scribens versiculos uterq̃ nostrum :

Plate 26. From · *Catullus: Poems.* Writing attributed to Ludovicus Regius. c.1495. Nat. Lib. of Scotland, Edinburgh (Adv. MS. 18.5.2).

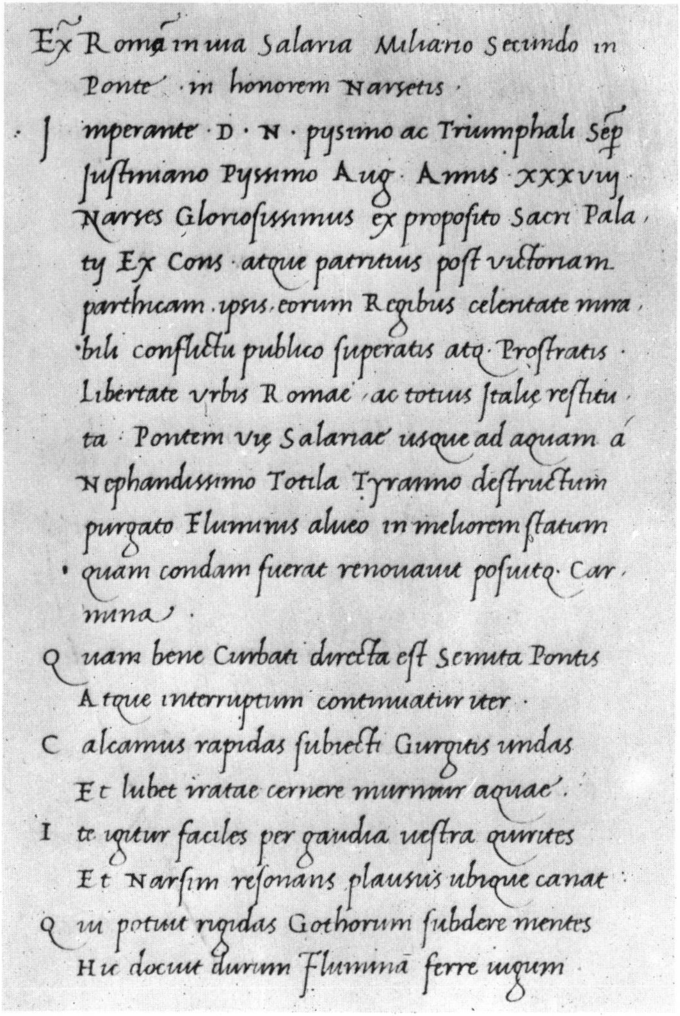

Ex Roma in uia Salaria Miliario secundo in
Ponte · in honorem Narsetis ·

I mperante · D · N · pyssimo ac Triumphali Sep
Justiniano Pyssimo Aug · Annis · XXXviij ·
Narses Gloriosissimus ex proposito Sacri Pala ·
ty Ex Cons · atque patricius post uictoriam.
parthicam · ipsis · eorum Regibus celeritate mira ·
·bili conflictu publico superatis atq; Prostratis ·
Libertate urbis Romae · ac totius Italię restitu ·
ta · Pontem uię Salariae usque ad aquam a
Nephandissimo Totila Tyranno destructum
purgato Fluminis alueo in meliorem statum
· quam condam fuerat renouauit posuitq; Car ·
mina ·

Q uam bene Curbati directa est Semita Pontis
A tque interruptum continuatur iter ·

C alcamus rapidas subiecti Gurgitis undas
E t lubet iratae cernere murmur aquae ·

I te igitur faciles per gaudia uestra quirites
E t Narsim resonans plausus ubique canat ·

Q ui potuit rigidas Gothorum subdere mentes
H ic docuit durum Flumina ferre iugum ·

Plate 27. From a collection of classical inscriptions written in Rome. *c.*1500.
(In the possession of Mrs James Wardrop.)

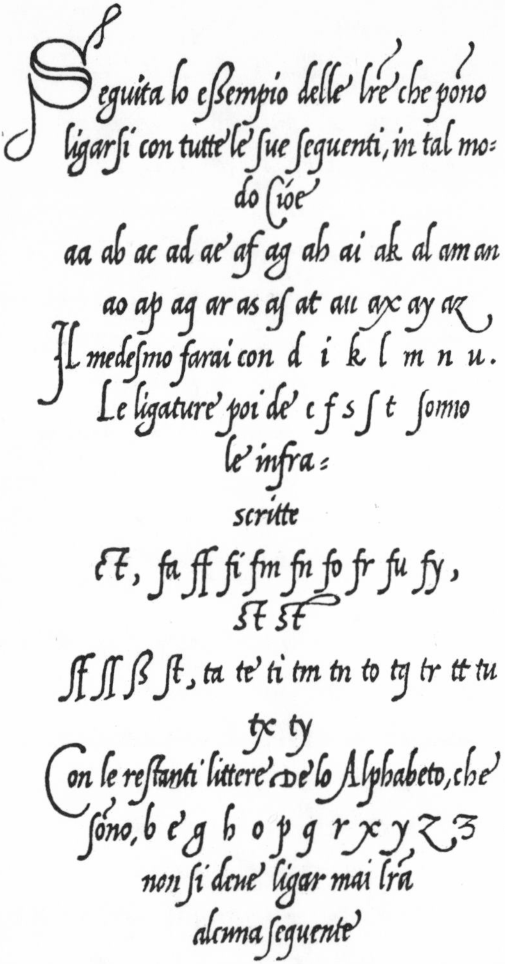

Seguita lo essempio delle lre che pono
ligarsi con tutte le sue sequenti, in tal mo=
do cioe

aa ab ac ad ae af ag ah ai ak al am an
ao ap aq ar as af at au ax ay az
Il medesmo farai con d i k l m n u.
Le ligature poi de c f s ſ t sonno
le infra =
scritte

et, fa ff fi fm fn fo fr fu fy,
ſt ſt

ſſ ſſ ß ſt, ta te ti tm tn to tq tr tt tu
tx ty
Con le restanti littere de lo Alphabeto, che
sono, b e g h o p q r x y z z
non si deue ligar mai lra
alcuna sequente

Plate 28. From *La Operina* by Ludovico degli Arrighi.
Rome, 1522.

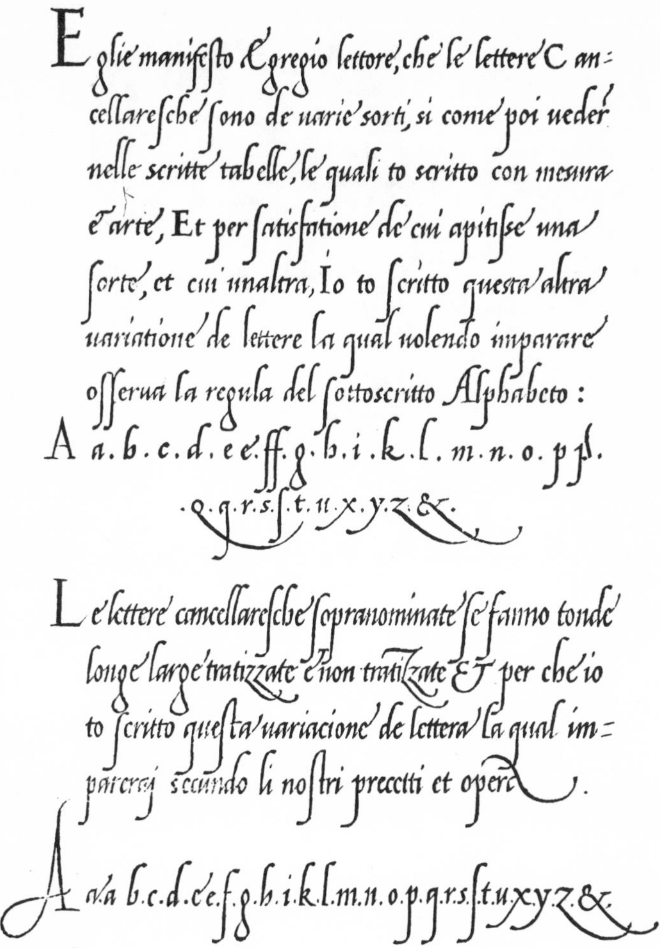

E glie manifesto Egregio lettore, che le lettere C an=
cellaresche sono de uarie sorti, si come poi ueder
nelle scritte tabelle, le quali to scritto con mesura
e arte, Et per satisfatione de cui apitise una
sorte, et cui unaltra, Io to scritto questa altra
uariatione de lettere la qual uolendo imparare
osserua la regula del sottoscritto Alphabeto :
A a. b. c. d. e e. ff. g. h. i. k. l. m. n. o. p s.
.o. q. r. s. s. t. u x. y. z. &.

L e lettere cancellaresche sopranominate se fanno tonde
longe large tratizzate e non tratizzate Et per che io
to scritto questa uariacione de lettera la qual im=
parerai secundo li nostri precetti et opera .

A da b. c. d. e. f. g. h. i. k. l. m. n. o. p. q. r. s. s. t. u x. y. z. &.

Plate 29. From *Opera che insegna a scrivere* by G. A. Tagliente. Venice, 1524.
V. and A.M.

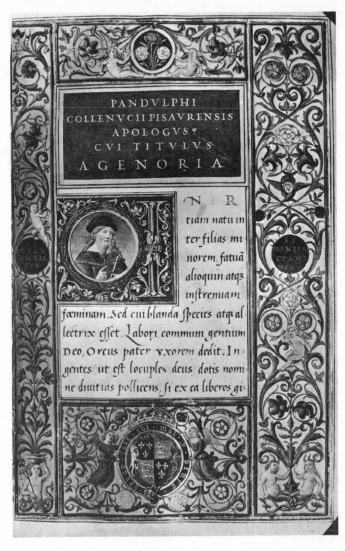

Plate 30. From *Apologues of Pandolfo Collenuccio*, etc. Writing attributed to Arrighi. *c*.1517. B.M. (Royal MS. 12. C. viii). The manuscript was presented to Henry VIII by Geoffrey Chamber.

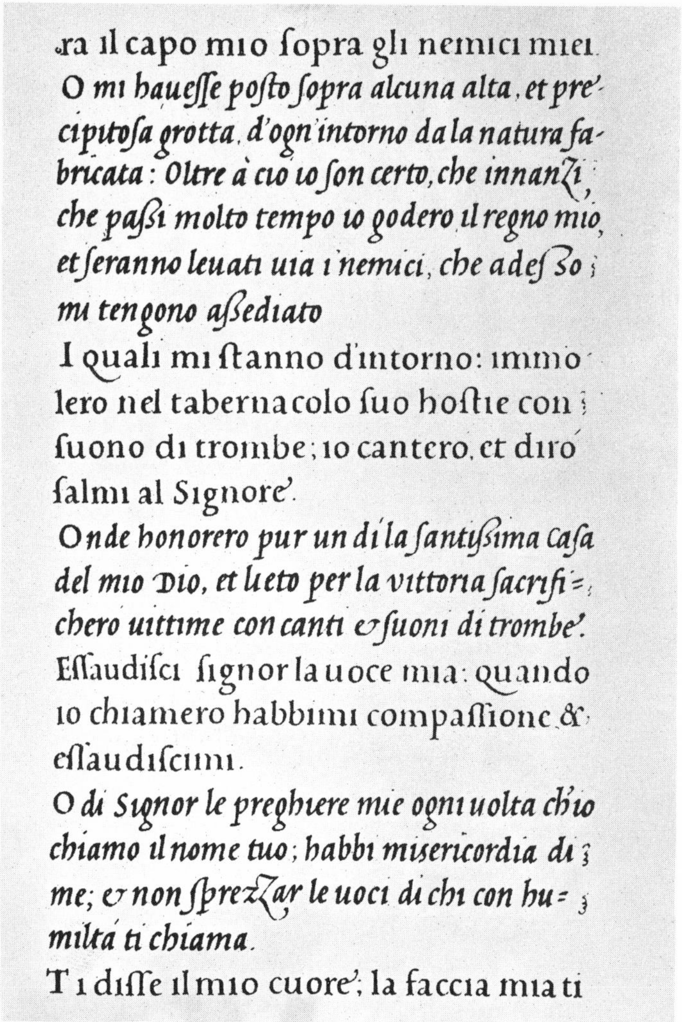

ra il capo mio sopra gli nemici miei.
O mi hauesse posto sopra alcuna alta, et pre-
cipitosa grotta, d'ogn'intorno da la natura fa-
bricata: Oltre à ciò io son certo, che innanzi
che passi molto tempo io godero il regno mio,
et seranno leuati uia i nemici, che adesso
mi tengono assediato

I quali mi stanno d'intorno: immo
lero nel tabernacolo suo hostie con
suono di trombe; io cantero, et dirò
salmi al Signore.

Onde honorero pur un dì la santissima Casa
del mio Dio, et lieto per la vittoria sacrifi=
chero uittime con canti e suoni di trombe.
Essaudisci signor la uoce mia: quando
io chiamero habbimi compassione &
essaudiscimi.

O di Signor le preghiere mie ogni uolta ch'io
chiamo il nome tuo; habbi misericordia di
me; e non sprezzar le uoci di chi con hu=
miltà ti chiama.

Ti disse il mio cuore, la faccia mia ti

Plate 31. From *La Paraphrasi* by Marcantonio Flaminio. Written in Italy
in the 16th century. B.M. (Harl. MS. 3451).

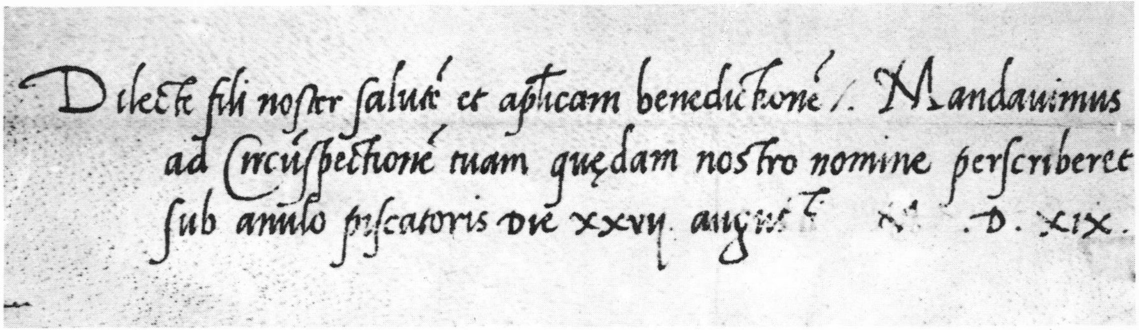

Dilecte fili noster salutē et apl[ic]am benedictionē ./. Mandauimus
ad Circumspectionē tuam quedam nostro nomine perscriberet
sub annulo piscatoris die xxvij. augusti M.D.XIX.

Plate 32. From a Papal Brief to Cardinal Wolsey dated 27 August 1519. Writing attributed to Ludovico degli Arrighi. P.R.O. (S.P. 19. f. 11).

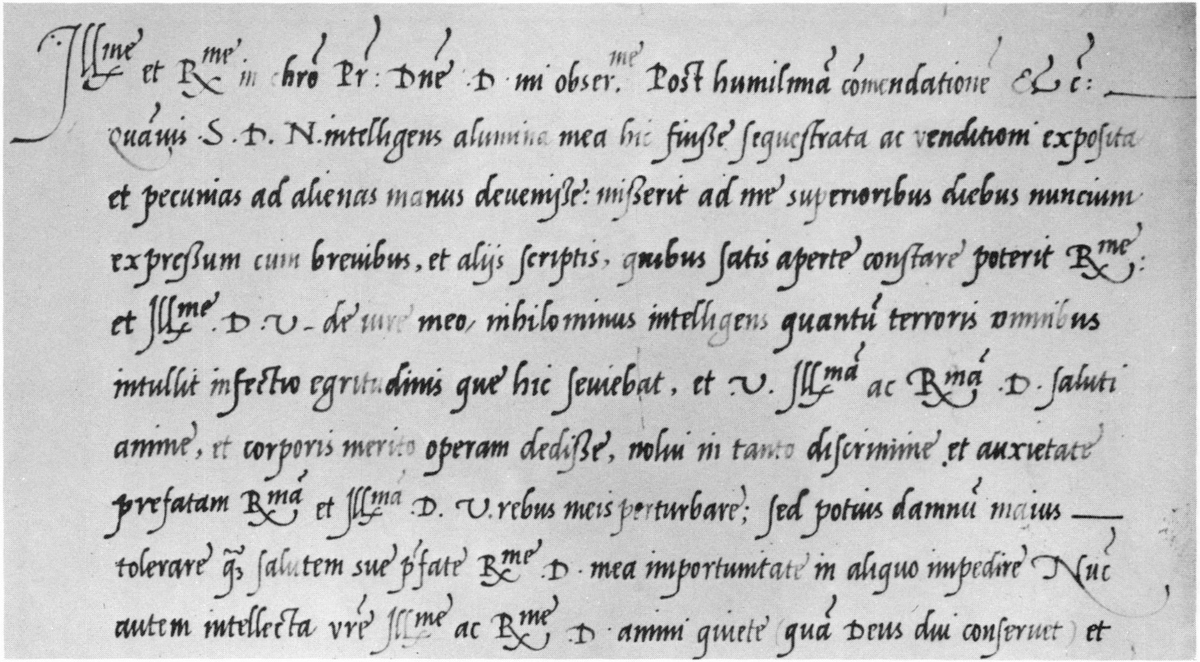

Illme et Rme in chro Pr: Dne D. mi obserme. Post humilima comendatione &c:
quamis S. D. N. intelligens alumina mea hic fuisse sequestrata ac venditiom exposita
et pecunias ad alienas manus devenisse: misserit ad me superioribus diebus nuncium
expressum cum brevibus, et aliis scriptis, quibus satis aperte constare poterit Rme:
et Illme. D. V. de iure meo, nihilominus intelligens quantu terroris omnibus
intullit infectio egritudinis que hic seviebat, et V. Illma ac Rma D. saluti
anime, et corporis merito operam dedisse, nolui in tanto discrimine et anxietate
prefatam Rma et Illma D. V. rebus meis perturbare; sed potius damnu maius
tolerare q̃ salutem sue pfate Rme D. mea importunitate in aliquo impedire Nunc
autem intellecta vre Illme ac Rme D. animi quiete (qua Deus diu conservet) et

Plate 33. From a letter to Cardinal Wolsey from Pasqual Spinula, a Genoese merchant of Shoreditch, written by a secretary. August 6th, 1528. P.R.O. (S.P. 1/49, f. 204).

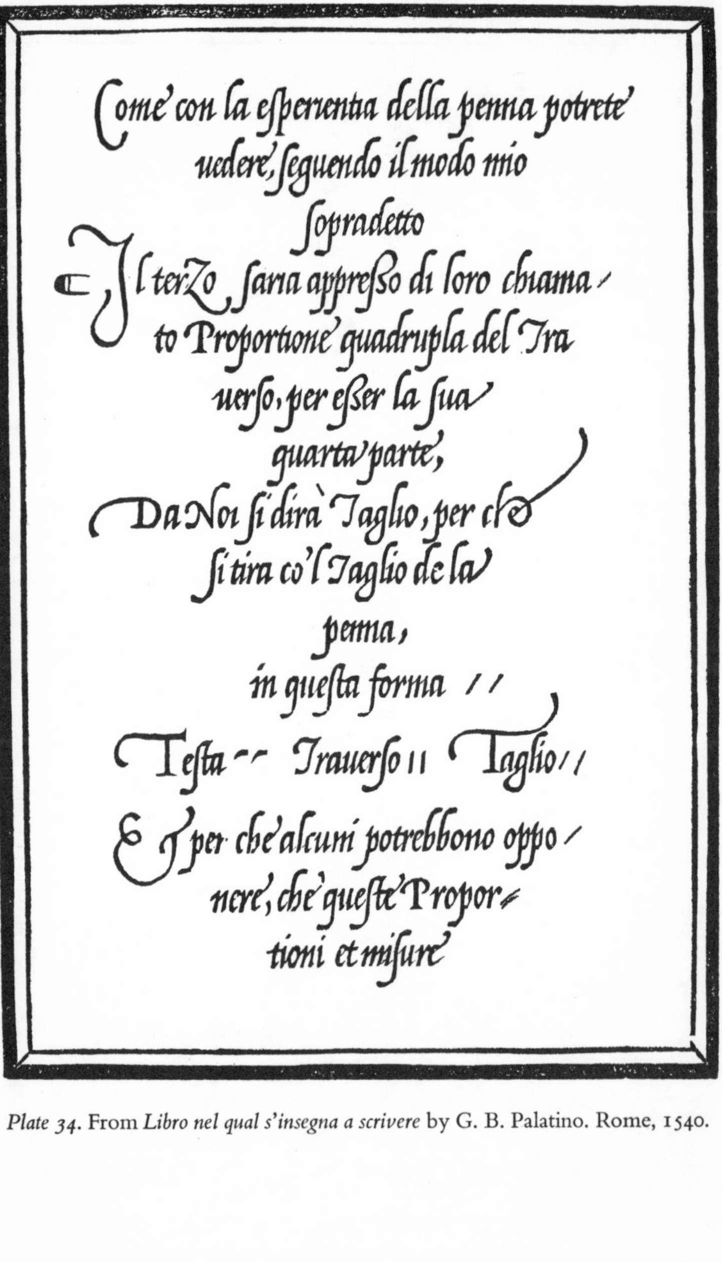

Come' con la esperientia della penna potrete'
uedere', seguendo il modo mio
sopradetto

Il terzo, saria appresso di loro chiama-
to Proportione' quadrupla del Tra
uerso, per esser la sua
quartav parte',

Da Noi si dirà Taglio, per ch
si tira co'l Taglio de la
penna,
in questa forma //

Testa -- Trauerso || Taglio //

E per che'alcuni potrebbono oppo-
nere', che' queste'Propor-
tioni et misure'

Plate 34. From *Libro nel qual s'insegna a scrivere* by G. B. Palatino. Rome, 1540.

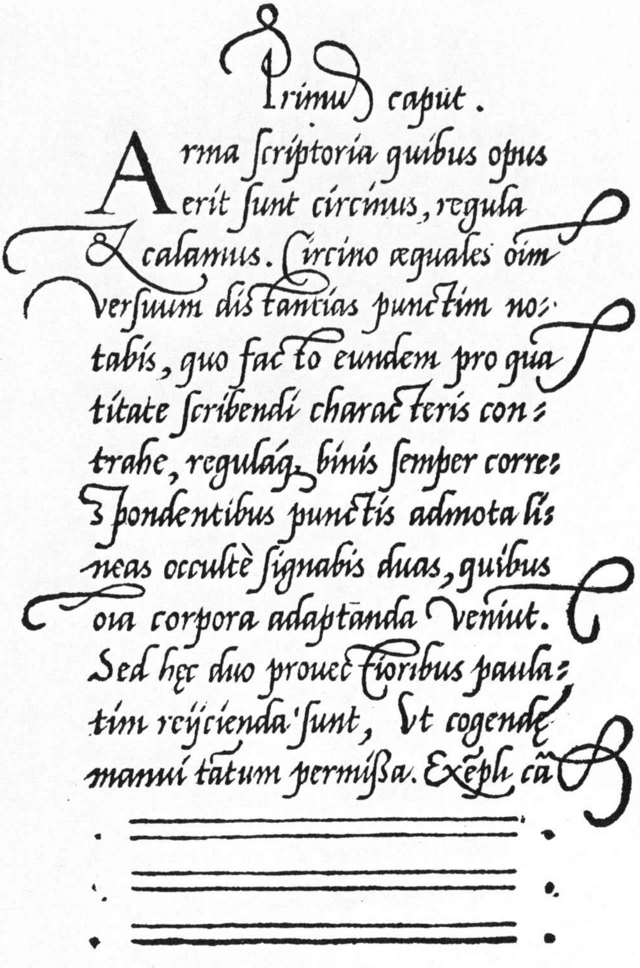

Primus) caput.

Arma scriptoria quibus opus
erit sunt circinus, regula
& calamus. Circino æquales oim
versuum distantias punctim no-
tabis, quo facto eundem pro qua
titate scribendi characteris con-
trahe, regulaq, binis semper corre-
spondentibus punctis admota li-
neas occultè signabis duas, quibus
oia corpora adaptanda veniut.
Sed hæc duo prouectioribus paula-
tim reijcienda sunt, vt cogendæ
manui tatum permissa. Exempli câ

Plate 35. From *Literarum Latinarum* by Gerard Mercator. Antwerp, 1540. B.M.
Mercator is the famous map-publisher, whose projection is still used.

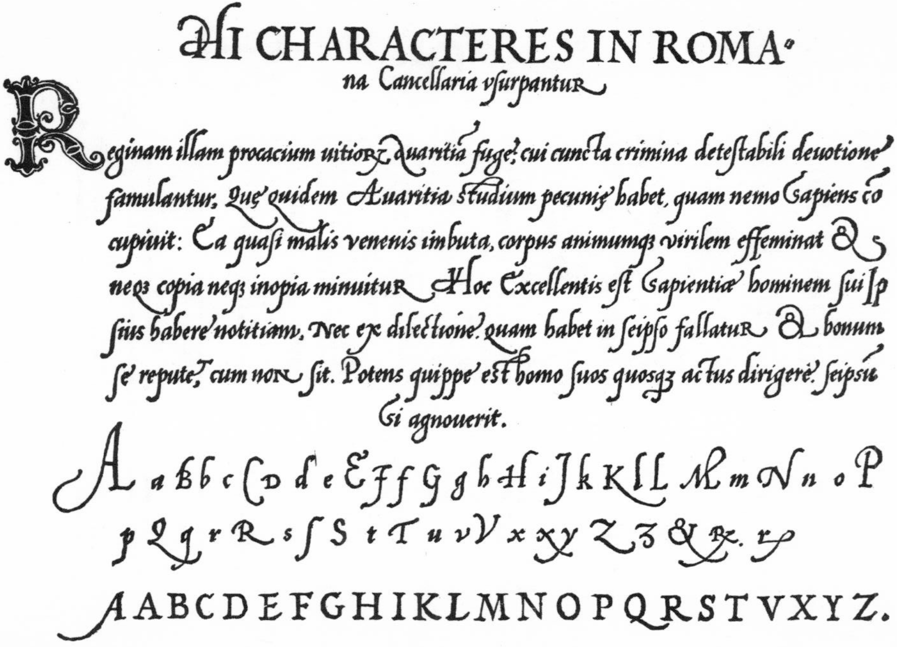

HI CHARACTERES IN ROMA.

na Cancellaria vsurpantur

Reginam illam præciuum vitiorꝝ auaritia fuget cui cuncta crimina detestabili deuotione famulantur, quæ quidem Auaritia studium pecuniæ habet, quam nemo sapiens co cupiuit: Ea quasi malis veneris imbuta, corpus animumqꝝ virilem effeminat ᵭ neqꝝ copia neqꝝ inopia minuitur. Hæc Excellentis est sapientiæ hominem sui ſp sius habere notitiam, nec ex directione quam habet in seipso fallatur, ᵭ hominum se reputet, cum nou sit. Potens quippe est homo suos quosqꝝ actus dirigere, seipsu Gi agnouerit.

A a B b C c D e E f F g G h H i J k K l L M m N n o P p Q q R s ſ S t T u v V x y Z ʒ & ꝝ ꝛ

A A B C D E F G H I K L M N O P Q R S T V X Y Z.

Plate 36. From Thesaurarium Artis Scriptoriæ by Caspar Neff. Cologne, 1549. V. and A.M.

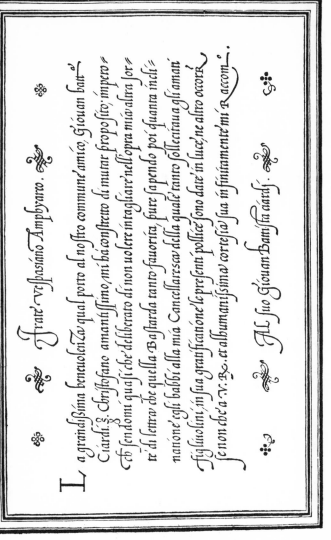

Plate 37. From *Opera nella quale si insegna a scrivere* by Vespasiano Amphiareo. Venice, 1554. V. and A. M.

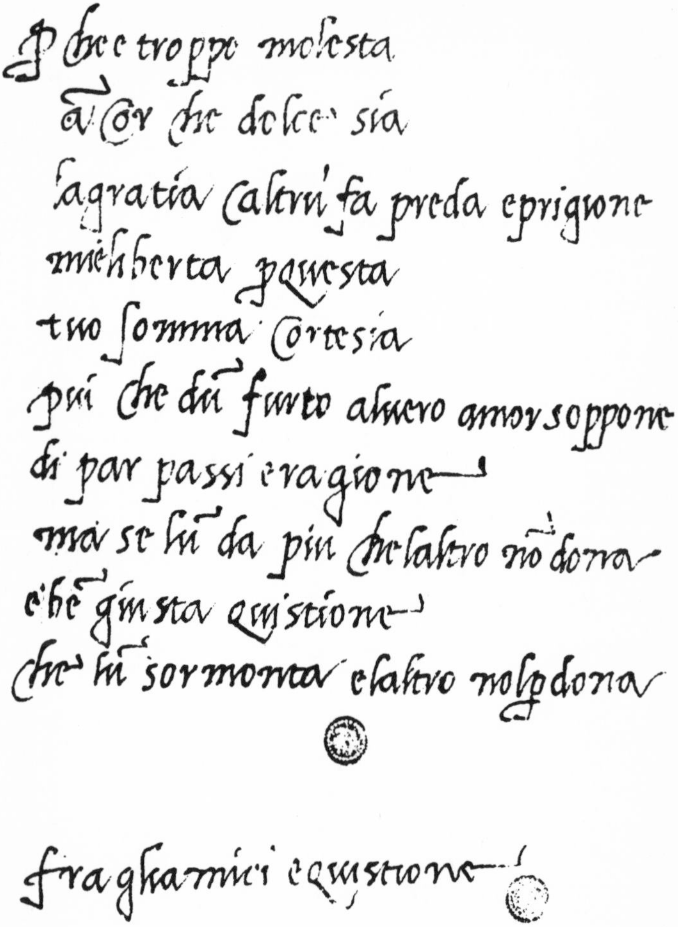
P che e troppo molesta
a cor che dolce sia
la gratia c'altrui fa preda e prigione
mie liberta per questa
tuo somma cortesia
piu che di furto al vero amor s'oppone
di par passi e ragione
ma se lu da piu che l'altro no dona
che e giusta quistione
che lu sormonta e l'altro nol perdona

fra gl'amici e quistione

Plate 38. Madrigal written by Michael Angelo.
(From *Renaissance Handwriting.*)

Sacratiss.ᵃ Ces. M.ᵗᵃ

Mandai alcuni mesi sono a v. M.ᵗᵃ per le mani del s. Don Dieg suo Ambasciator il ritratto
della s. memoria della Imp.ᶜᵉ sua consorte fatto di mia mano con qllaltro che mi fu dato
da lei per essempio. Ma perche tutte le mie uoglie di q'sto mondo nõ sono altro che uno ar-
dentiss.ᵉ disiderio di seruire et sodisfare in cio che io posso a v. M.ᵗᵃ Sto con infinita deuotiõe
aspettando dintendere se q'sta mia opera le sia giunta inanzi, et se le sia piaciuta, o nõ .
Che se io sapero eserle piaciuta, ne sentiro ᵱal contento nellanimo, cʰ nõ son bastante a dirlo :
et se ancho sara il contrario. io mi proferisco di racconciarla in maniera che v. M.ᵗᵃ se ne conten-
terà, quãdo N. S. Dio mi donera gratia di poter io uenire a presentarle una figura di Venere
da me fatta a nome suo : Laqual figura ho speranza che fara chiara fede' quanto la mia
arte auanzi se stessa in adoperarsi per la M. v. Io sono hora qui in Roma chiamatoci
da N. S. et uado imparando da q'sti marauigliosiss. salsi antichi cose per leq'li larte mia
diuenghi degna di pingere le uittorie che N. S. Dio prepara a v. M.ᵗᵃ in oriente .
In tanto uol' bascio la inuittissima mano con tutto laffetto et reuerentia del mio cuore' : et la
supplico che si degni cõmettere' et fare', che la tratta de i grani del Regno di Napoli dona-
tami tanti anni sono dalla v. M.ᵗᵃ et la pensione delli cento scuti, che ella ordinò cʰ mi
fosse pagata ognianno in Milano per cagiõ della Nonciata che io le presentai, habbia effetto :
che ne luna, ne laltra io ho mai hauuto fin qui, senza saputa di v. M.ᵗᵃ .
Di Roma alli viij. di Decembre. M. D x L V.

Di v. Ces. M.ᵗᵃ

Humilliss.ᵃ creatura e seruo

Titiano Pittore' /

Plate 39. From a letter signed Titian Pittore (Titian) to Charles V. December 8th,
1545. (Whereabouts unknown.)

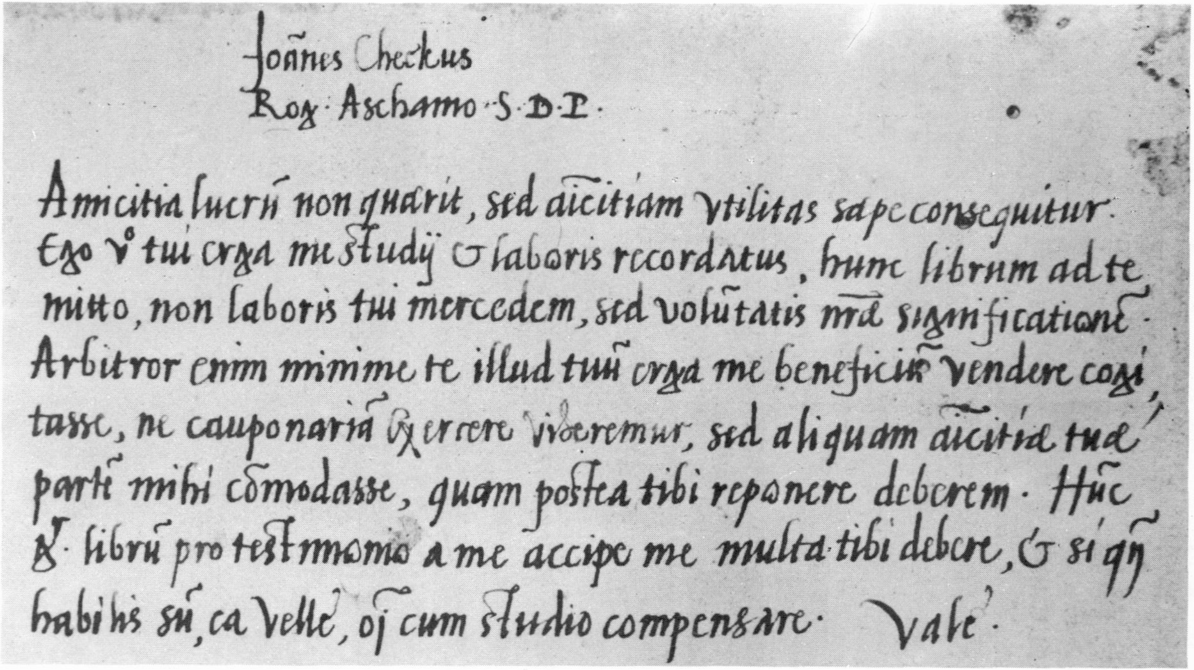

Joannes Checkus
Rog. Aschamo S. D. P.

Amicitia lucrum non quaerit, sed amicitiam utilitas saepe consequitur. Ego vero tui erga me studii & laboris recordatus, hunc librum ad te mitto, non laboris tui mercedem, sed voluntatis meae significationem. Arbitror enim minime te illud tuum erga me beneficium vendere cogitasse, ne cauponariam exercere videremur, sed aliquam amicitiae tuae partem mihi commodasse, quam postea tibi reponere deberem. Hunc igitur librum pro testimonio a me accipe me multa tibi debere, & si quando habilis sim, ea velle, omnia cum studio compensare. Vale.

Plate 40. Presentation inscription written by Sir John Cheke to Roger Ascham. Undated.
St John's College, Cambridge (Aa.1.51).

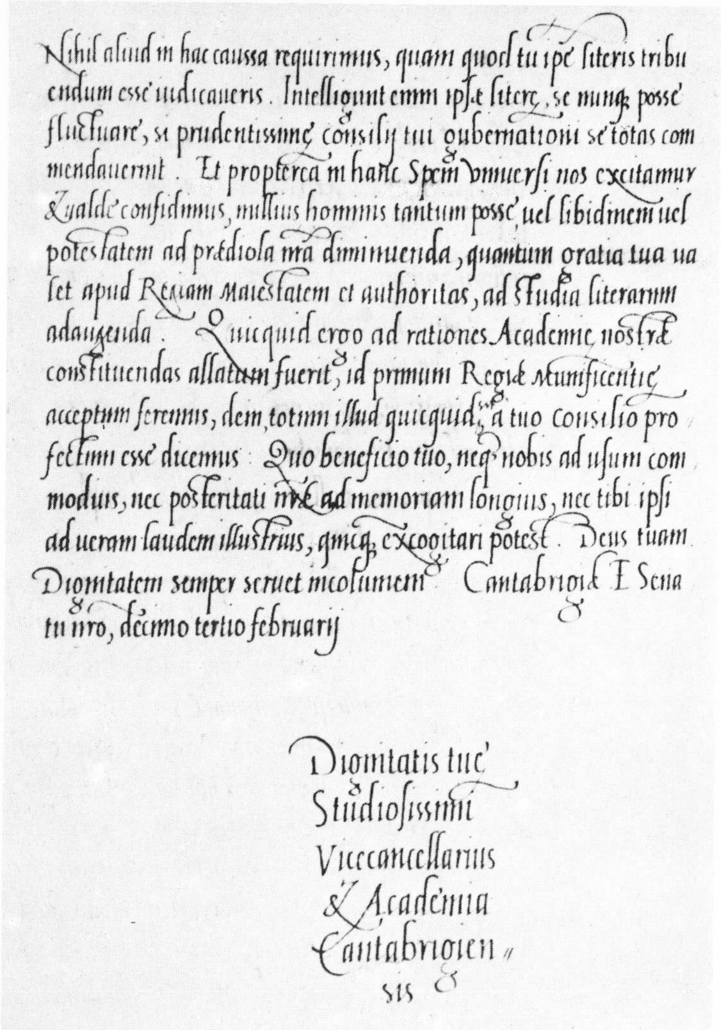

Nihil aliud in hac caussa requirimus, quam quod tu ipse literis tribu
endum esse iudicaueris. Intelligunt enim ipsę literę, se nunqz posse
fluctuare, si prudentissime consilij tui gubernationi se totas com
mendauerint. Et propterea in hanc Spem vniuersi nos excitamur
& valde confidimus, nullius hominis tantum posse, uel libidinem uel
potestatem ad prędiola nra diminuenda, quantum oratia tua ua
let apud Regiam Maiestatem et authoritas, ad studia literarum
adaugenda. Quicquid ergo ad rationes Academię nostrę
constituendas allatum fuerit, id primum Regię Munificentię
acceptum feremus, dein, totum illud quicquid, a tuo Consilio pro
fectum esse dicemus. Quo beneficio tuo, neqz nobis ad usum com
modius, nec posteritati nrę ad memoriam longius, nec tibi ipsi
ad ueram laudem illustrius, qmcqz excogitari potest. Deus tuam
Dignitatem semper seruet incolumem. Cantabrigię I Sena
tu nro, decimo tertio februarij

                    Dignitatis tuę
                    Studiosissimi
                    Viceancellarius
                    & Academia
                    Cantabrigien-
                        sis

Plate 41. From a letter from Cambridge University to Sir Wm Paget written
by Roger Ascham. February 13th, 1545/6. P.R.O. (S.P. 1/214, f. 54).

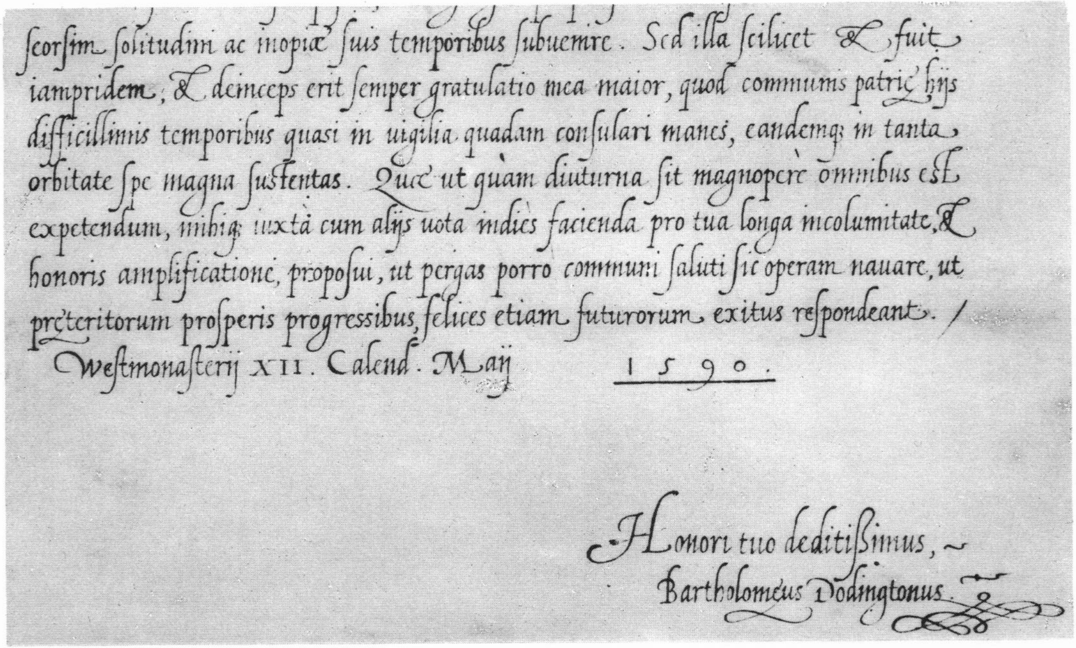

seorsim solitudini ac inopiæ suis temporibus subuenire. Sed illa scilicet & fuit iampridem, & deinceps erit semper gratulatio mea maior, quod communis patriæ suis difficillimis temporibus quasi in uigilia quadam consulari manes, eandemq in tanta orbitate spe magna sustentas. Quæ ut quam diuturna sit magnopere omnibus est expetendum, inibiq iuxtà cum aliis uota indies facienda pro tua longa incolumitate, & honoris amplificatione, proposui, ut peragas porro communi saluti sic operam nauare, ut præteritorum prosperis progressibus, felices etiam futurorum exitus respondeant. /
Westmonasterij XII. Calend. Maij

1 5 9 0.

Amori tuo deditissimus, ~
Bartholomeus Dodingtonus.

Plate 42. From a letter from Bartholomew Dodington to Lord Burleigh. May 12th, 1590. B.M. (Lansdowne 63).

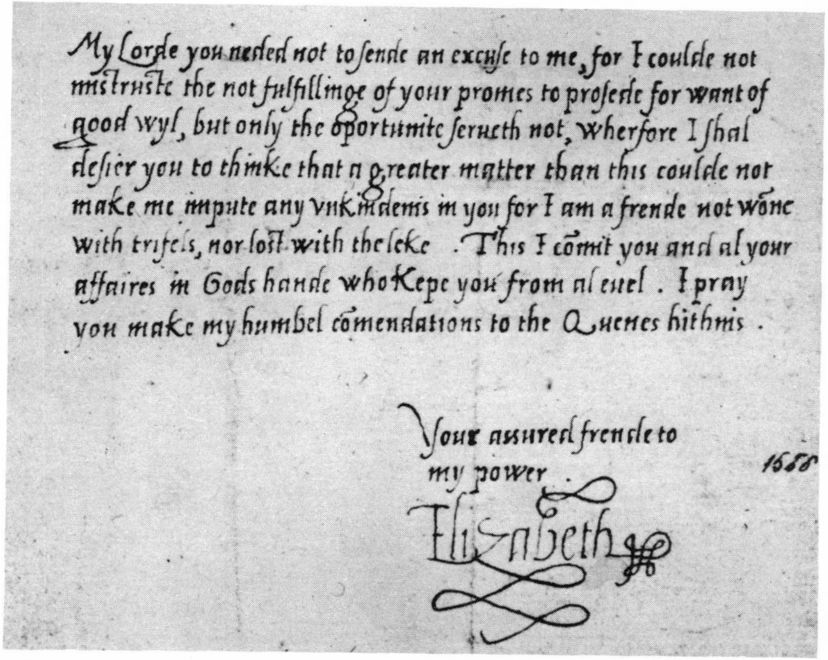

My Lorde you neded not to sende an excuse to me, for I coulde not mistruste the not fulfillinge of your promis to procede for want of good wyl, but only the oportunite serueth not, wherfore I shal desier you to thinke that a greater matter than this coulde not make me impute any vnkindenes in you for I am a frende not won with trifels, nor lost with thicke. This I commit you and al your affaires in Gods hande who kepe you from al euel. I pray you make my humbel comendations to the Quenes hithnis.

Your assured frende to
my power.
Elisabeth

Plate 43. A letter written by Elizabeth I, when a Princess, to Thomas Seymour. 1548. Pierpont Morgan Library, New York (Thane-Paston Collection).

Plate 44. From *Arte Subtilissima* by Juan de Yciar. Saragossa, 1555.
V. and A.M.

Plate 45. From *Arte de escrivir* by Francisco Lucas. Madrid, 1577.
V. and A.M.

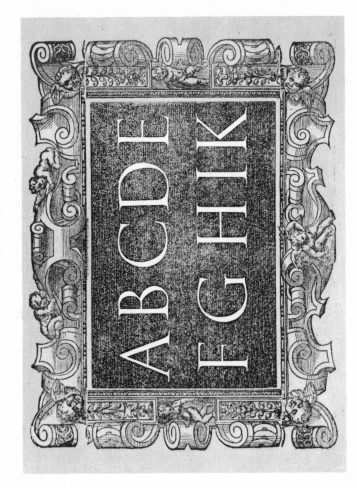

Plate 46. From *Il perfetto Scrittore* by G. F. Cresci. Venice, 1569. B.M.

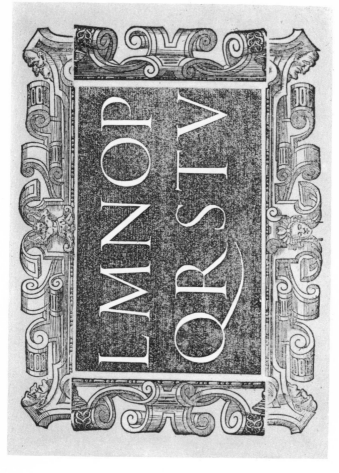

Plate 47. From *Il perfetto Scrittore* by G. F. Cresci. Venice, 1569. B.M.

Plate 48. From *Il perfetto Scrittore* by G. F. Cresci. Venice, 1569. B.M.

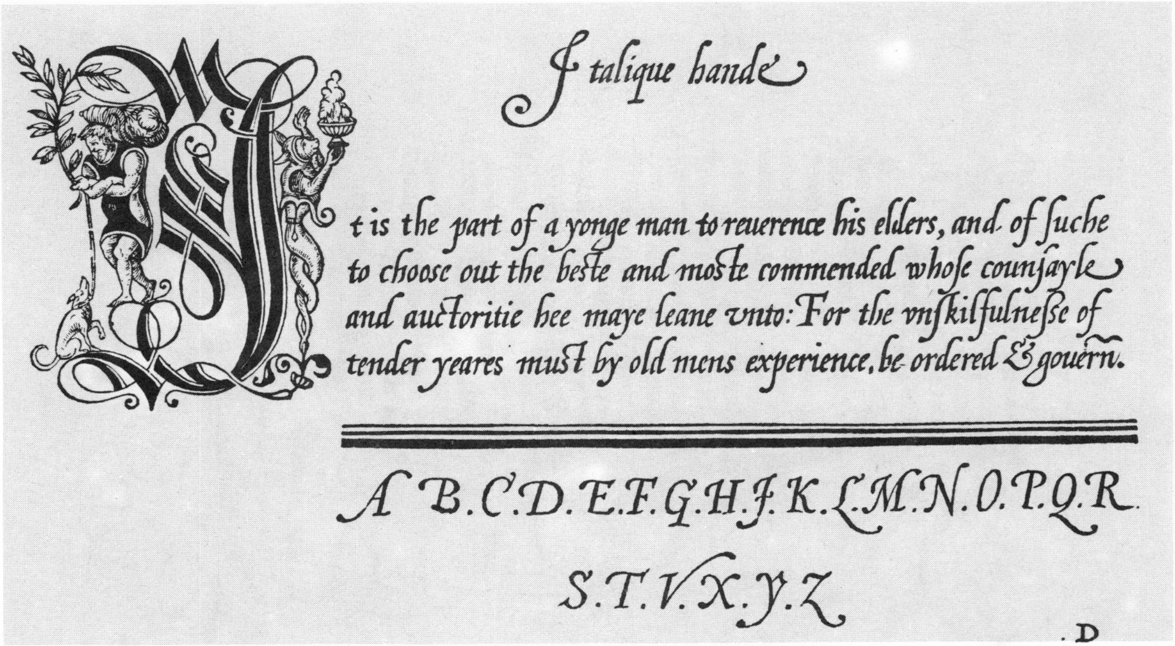

Italique hande

t is the part of a yonge man to reuerence his elders, and of suche
to chose out the beste and moste commended whose counsayle
and auctoritie hee maye leane vnto: For the vnskilfulnesse of
tender yeares must by old mens experience, be ordered & gouern.

A.B.C.D.E.F.G.H.F.K.L.M.N.O.P.Q.R.
S.T.V.X.Y.Z.

.D

Plate 49. From *A Booke Containing Divers Sortes of Hands* by Jean de Beauchesne and John Baildon. London, 1570. B.M.

Plate 50. From *A Booke Containing Divers Sortes of Hands* by Jean de Beauchesne and John Baildon. London, 1570, B.M. (Originally shown in *Ein neuw Fundamentbuch* by Urban Wyss. Zurich, 1562).

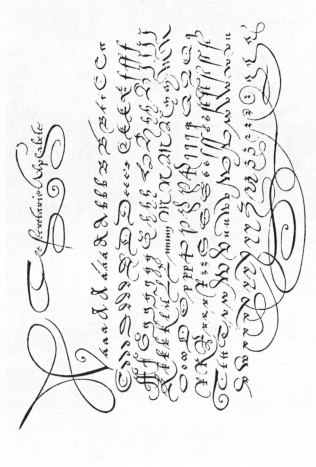

Plate 51. From *A Booke Containing Divers Sortes of Hands* by Jean de Beauchesne and John Baildon. London, 1570. B.M.

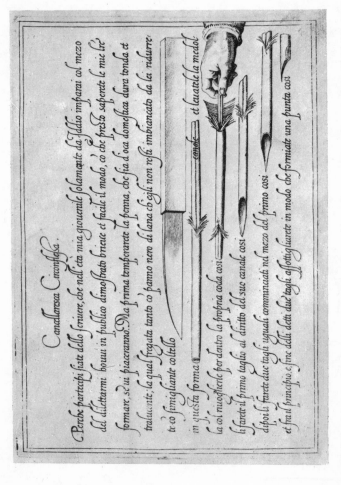

Candaresa Cancellesa.

Perche partecipi siate dello scriuere, che nell'età mia giouenile solamente da Iddio imparai col mezo dell'dilettarmi: bouui in publico dimostrato breuice et facile il modo, co che presto saperete le mie tre formar, s'vi piaceranno. Ma prima temperarete la penna, che sia d'oua domestica dura tonda et traluente, la qual fregata tanto co panno nero di lana ch'egli non resti imbrancato da la ridurre: tre co simigliante coltello

in questa forma.

la col muoglierle per dentro la propria coda così

sifarete il primo taglio al diritto del suo canale così

dipoi li farete due tagli uguali communicati nel mezo del primo così

et in al principio, e fine delli detti due tagli assottigliarete in modo che formiate una punta così

canole. *et lauatele la medol.*

Plate 52. From Lo Scritor' Utile et brieve Segretario *by G. A. Hercolani. Bologna, 1574. V. and A.M.*

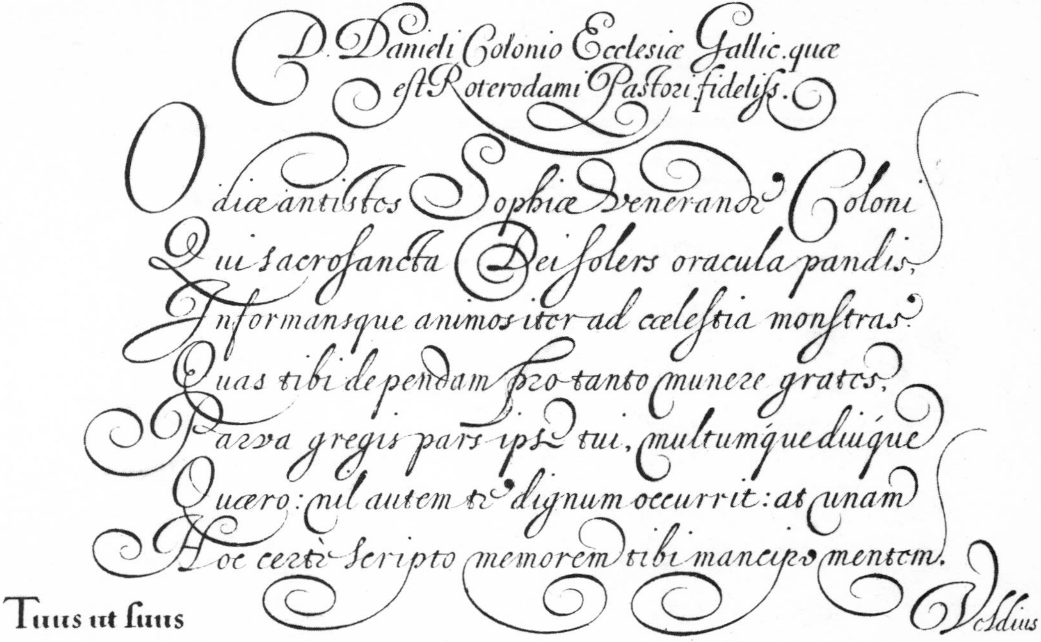

Plate 53. Part of a page from *Spieghel der Schrijfkonste* by Jan van den Velde. Rotterdam, 1605. V. and A. M. Flourished border omitted.

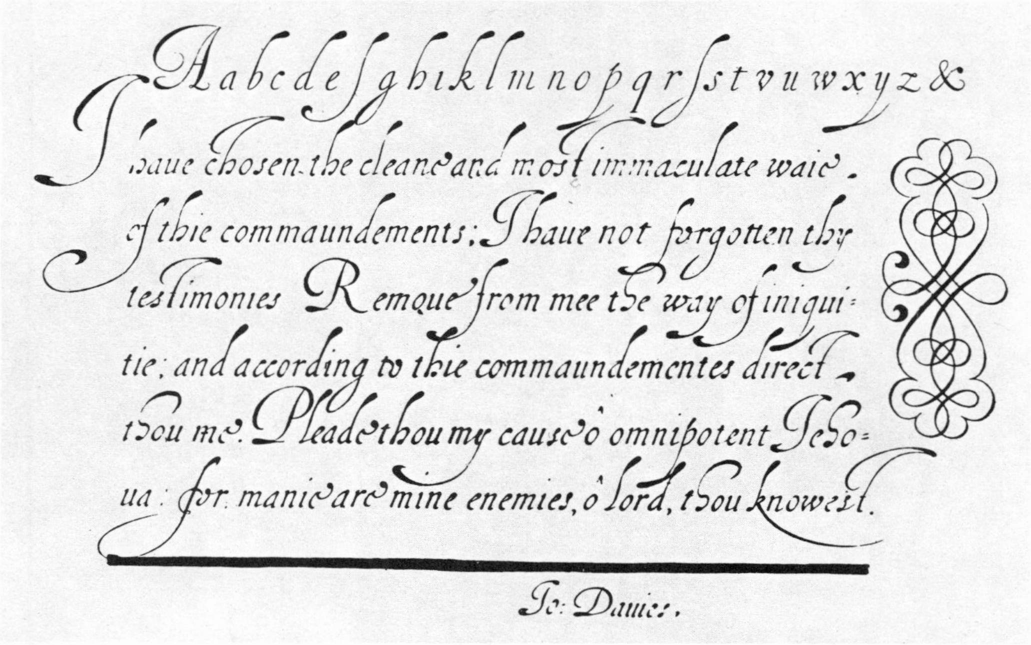

A a b c d e f g h i k l l m n o p q r s t v u w x y z &

haue chosen the cleane and most immaculate waie.
of thie commaundements: I haue not forgotten thy
testimonies. Remoue from mee the way of iniqui-
tie; and according to thie commaundementes direct
thou me. Pleade thou my cause, o omnipotent Ieho-
ua: for manie are mine enemies, o lord, thou knowest.

Io: Dauis.

Plate 54. From *The Writing Schoolmaster or the Anatomy of Faire Writing* by John Davies of Hereford. London, 1663. B.M. (John Davies: b. ?1565, d.1618.)

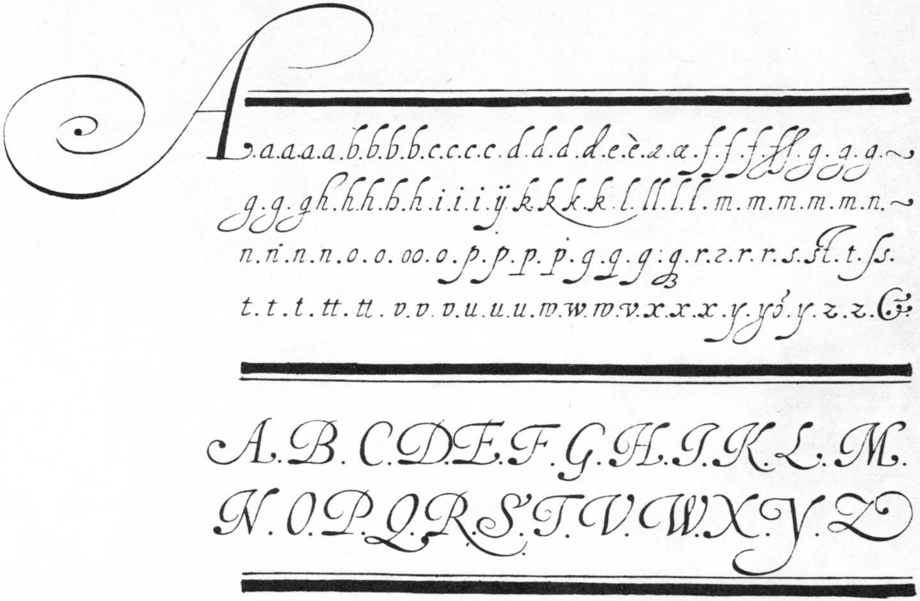

Plate 55. From Pens Excellencie or the Secretaries Delight by Martin Billingsley. London, 1618. (Billingsley: b.1591, d.1622.)

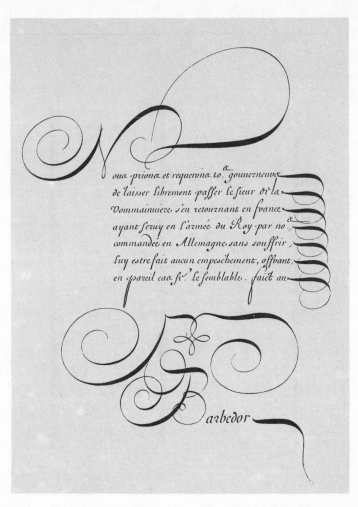

oua prions et requerons to.ᵉ gouuerneurs
de laisser librement passer le sieur ᵭ la
Vommainuiere s'en retournant en fvance
ayant feruy en l'armeé du Roy par no.ᵉ
commandeé en Allemagne sans souffrir
luy estre fait aucun empeschement, offrant
en spareil cas fi.ᵉ le semblable. faict au

a.rbedor

Plate 56. From *Les Ecritures Financière, et Italiennę-Bastarde* by
Louis Barbedor. Paris, 1647. B.M.

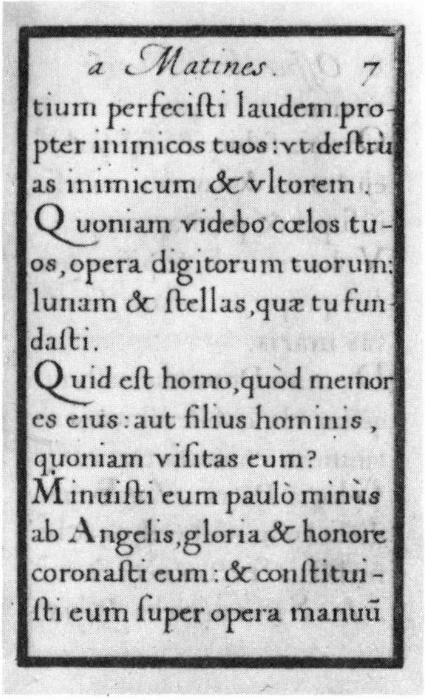

a Matines. 7
tium perfeciſti laudem pro-
pter inimicos tuos: vt deſtrù
as inimicum & vltorem.
Quoniam videbo cœlos tu-
os, opera digitorum tuorum:
lunam & ſtellas, quæ tu fun-
daſti.
Quid eſt homo, quòd memor
es eius: aut filius hominis,
quoniam viſitas eum?
Minuiſti eum paulò minùs
ab Angelis, gloria & honore
coronaſti eum: & conſtitui-
ſti eum ſuper opera manuū

Plate 57. From MS. *Office de la Vièrge à Matines*. Writing by Nicolas Jarry. Paris, 1659. B.M. (Add. MS. 39642).

Arme thy selfe against Temptations knowing they are a Christians portion in this Life In all thy affaires First aske Councell of God, and then go on in humility; ascribing the power and praise of all to God least He curse thy best doeings.

DISCE Pati.

Prostant Æterna

Chorus

Plate 58. From *A Compendium of the Usuall Hands* written and invented by Richard Daniel and engraved by Edward Cocker. London, 1664. In the possession of Jan Tschichold.

A a b c d e ff fff ffg h h i k l ll m n o p p
Q q r s sf s tt ts v u w x y z æ

Let every day produce some curious Lines
That may commend thy Genius, & thy Pen.
Let all thy Undertakings and Designes
Tend to Gods Glory, and the good of men.

Cocker
A B C D E F G H I K L M N
O P Q R S T V V W X Y Z

Plate 59. From *Magnum in Parvo or the Pens Perfection*. Invented, written, and engraved in silver by Edward Cocker. London, 1672. V. and A.M.

Plate 60. From *Nuncius Oris: A Round-hand Coppy-book.* Invented, written, and engraved by Caleb Williams. London, 1593 (but probably intended to be 1693). B.M.

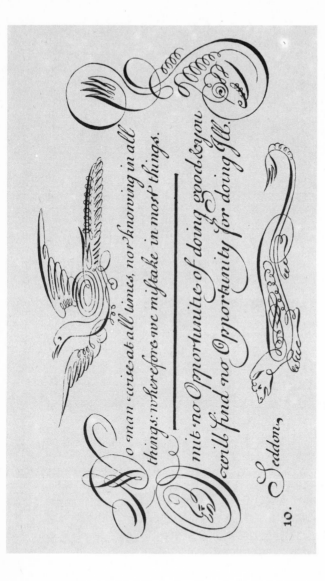

Plate 61. From *The Ingenious Youth's Companion* by John Seddon. London, 1698. V. and A.M. (Seddon: b.1644. d.1700).

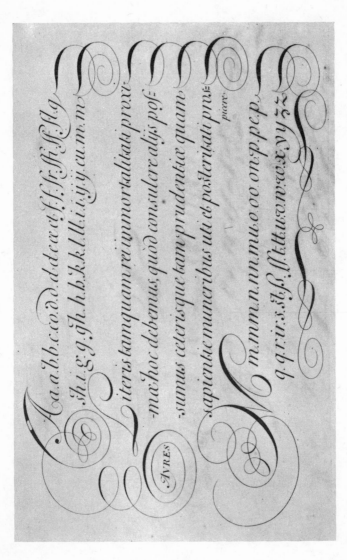

Plate 62. From *A Tutor to Penmanship* by John Ayres. 1698. B.M. (John Ayres: fl.1680–1705).

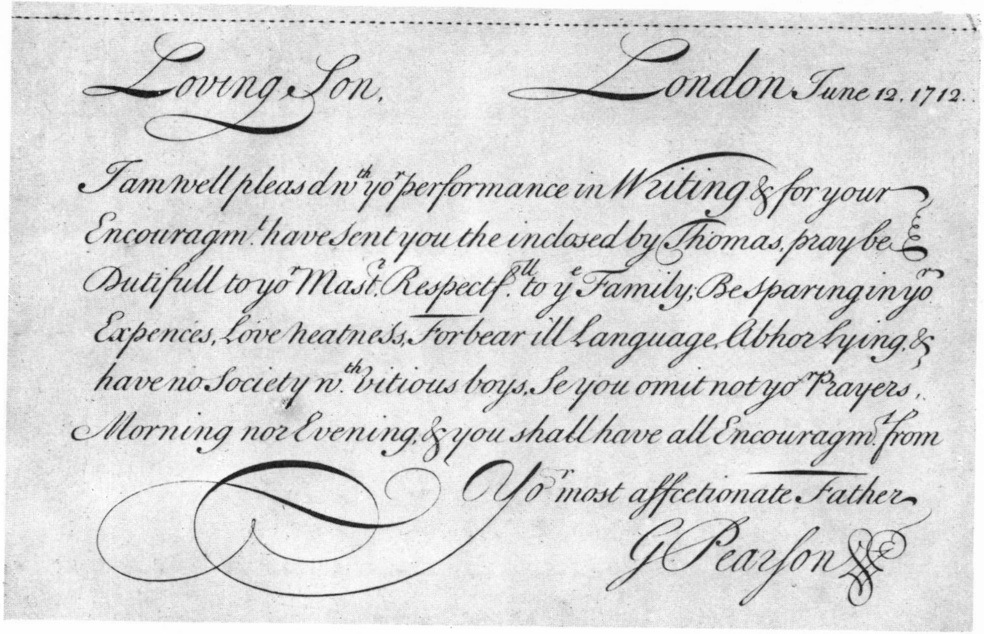

London June 12. 1712.

Loving Son,

I am well pleas'd w.th yo.r performance in Writing & for your Encouragm.t have sent you the inclosed by Thomas, pray be Dutifull to yo.r Mast. Respectf.ll to y.e Family; Be sparing in yo.r Expences, Love neatness, Forbear ill Language, & thoe living & have no society w.th vitious boys, Se you omit not yo.r Prayers. Morning nor Evening & you shall have all Encouragm.t from

Yo.r most affectionate Father

G Pearson

Plate 63. Part of a page of *Penmanship in its Utmost Beauty* by George Bickham the Elder. London, 1731. V. and A.M. Example written by George Shelley and engraved by Bickham. (Shelley: b. ?1666, d. ?1736).

Tis. very advantagious for ingenuous men
to communicate their sentiments to each
other it discovers a generosity. improves
the judgement. invigorates the fancy. cre-
ates emulation. and promotes industry.

Plate 64. Part of a page of *Art of Writing* by Charles Snell. London, 1712. V. and A.M. Engraved by G. Bickham. (Snell: b.1667, d.1733). The copy-book was arranged so that it could be cut up into about one hundred pieces. The plate shows two parts, the flourish being one.

Education strikes in with Philosophy in many lessons; teaches us not to be over-joyd in Prosperity, nor too much dejected in Adversity; not to be dissolute in our Pleasures, nor in our Anger to be transported to a Fury that is Brutal. Wxyz

Plate 65. Part of a page of *The Universal Penman* by George Bickham the Elder. London, 1733–41. V. and A.M. (Bickham: b. ?1684, d. ?1758). The specimen shown was possibly engraved by Bickham from his own writing.

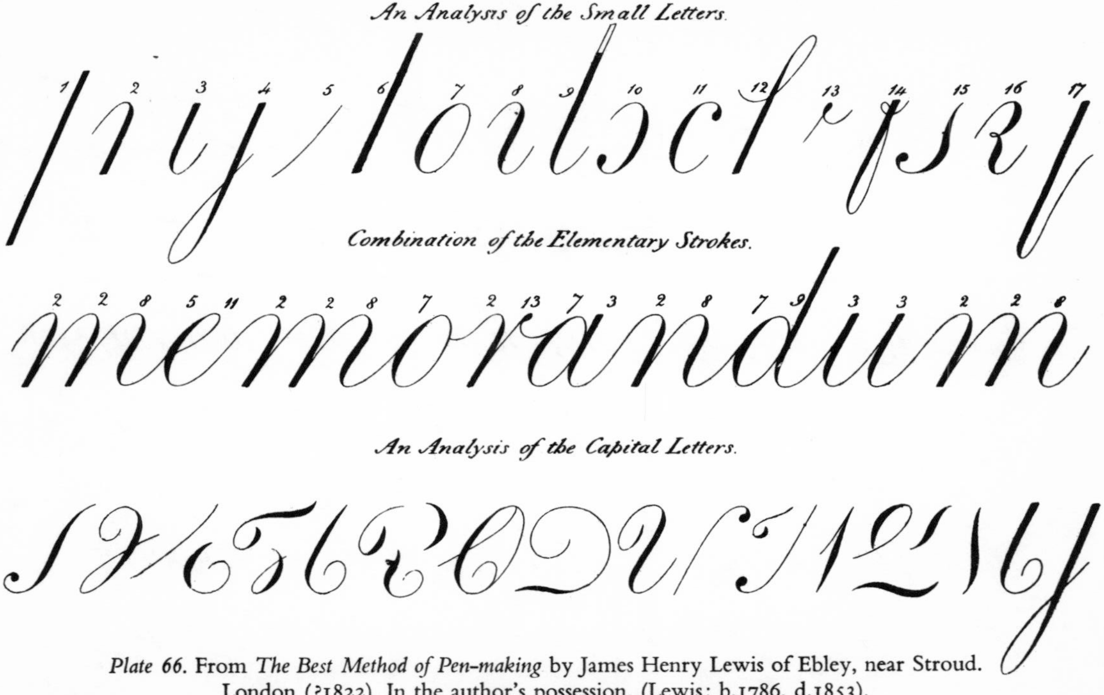

An Analysis of the Small Letters.

Combination of the Elementary Strokes.

memorandum

An Analysis of the Capital Letters.

Plate 66. From *The Best Method of Pen-making* by James Henry Lewis of Ebley, near Stroud. London (?1822). In the author's possession. (Lewis: b.1786, d.1853).

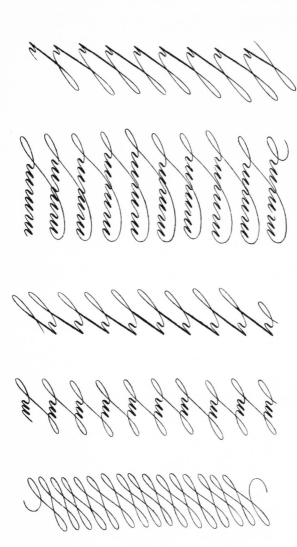

Plate 67. From *Lectures on the Art of Writing* by J. Carstairs. London, 1814. In the possession of B. L. Wolpe.

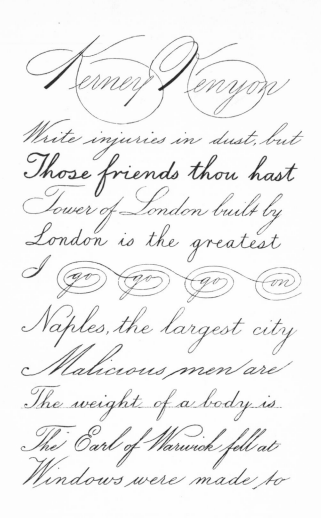

Plate 68. From *The Theory and Practice of Handwriting* by John Jackson. London, 1898. These examples, 11 of 73, had been culled by Jackson from a number of unspecified 19th-century head-line copy books. Jackson himself wrote and advocated a vertical hand.

18 Roman Road,
Bedford,
5th June

My dear Father,

The School and other examinations are now over, and I am first in Arithmetic, and second in History. I have also got the first prize for Writing.

The Holidays begin on Thursday, and though I like School I am only too glad to be returning home, and am longing to see you all again.

Your affectionate son,
William Deanham.

George Deanham Esq.

Plate 69. From the Vere Foster *New Civil Service Copy-book* (Medium Series). Messrs Blackie & Sons, Ltd, 1898.

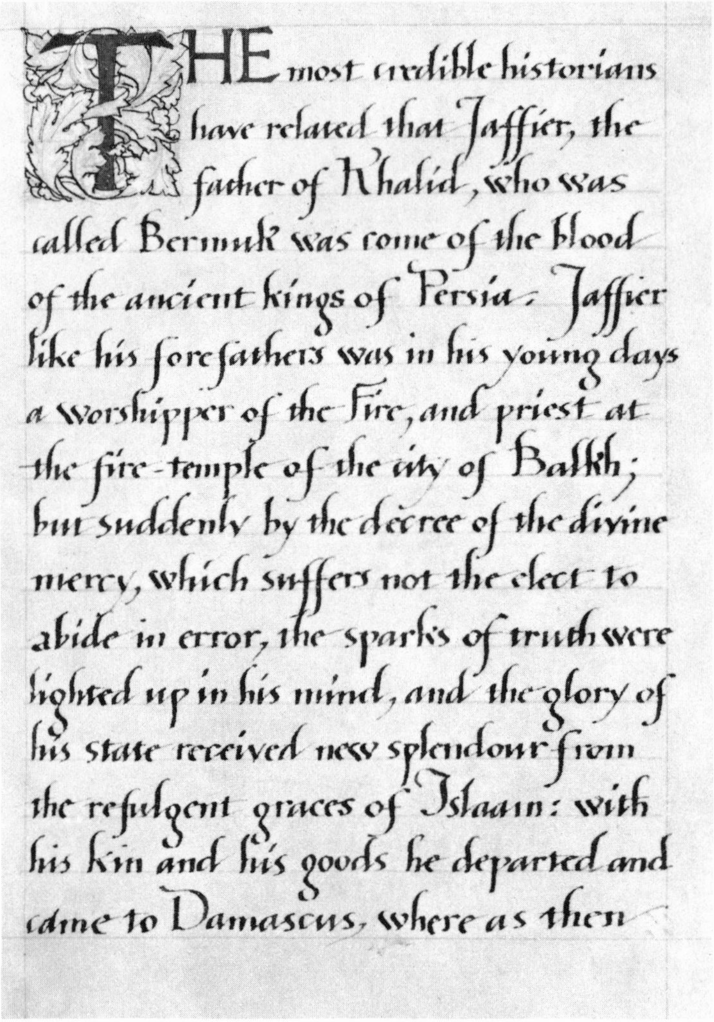

THE most credible historians have related that Jaffier, the father of Khalid, who was called Bermuk was come of the blood of the ancient kings of Persia: Jaffier like his forefathers was in his young days a worshipper of the fire, and priest at the fire-temple of the city of Balkh; but suddenly by the decree of the divine mercy, which suffers not the elect to abide in error, the sparks of truth were lighted up in his mind, and the glory of his state received new splendour from the refulgent graces of Islaain: with his kin and his goods he departed and came to Damascus, where as then

Plate 70. A set italic hand written by William Morris: *The Arabian Nights.*
?1875. B.L. (MS. Eng. Misc. d. 265, f.6r).

Come & sit under my stone pine that
murmurs so honey sweet as it bends to
the soft western breeze ; & lo this honey
dropping fountain, where I bring sweet
sleep, playing on my lonely reeds —

Plate 71. Part of a page of *A New Handwriting for Teachers* by
Mrs M. M. Bridges. Oxford University Press. First published 1898.

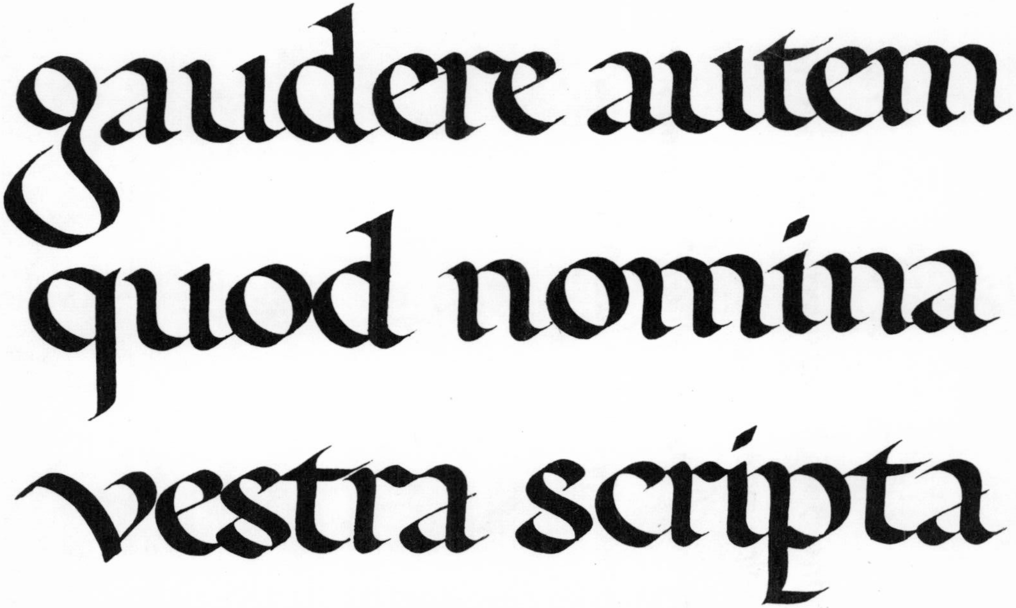

gaudere autem
quod nomina
vestra scripta

Plate 72. Part of a copy-sheet written by Edward Johnston on 27 August 1919. See note on *Plate 10.* The inscription closed with the words *sunt in coelis.*

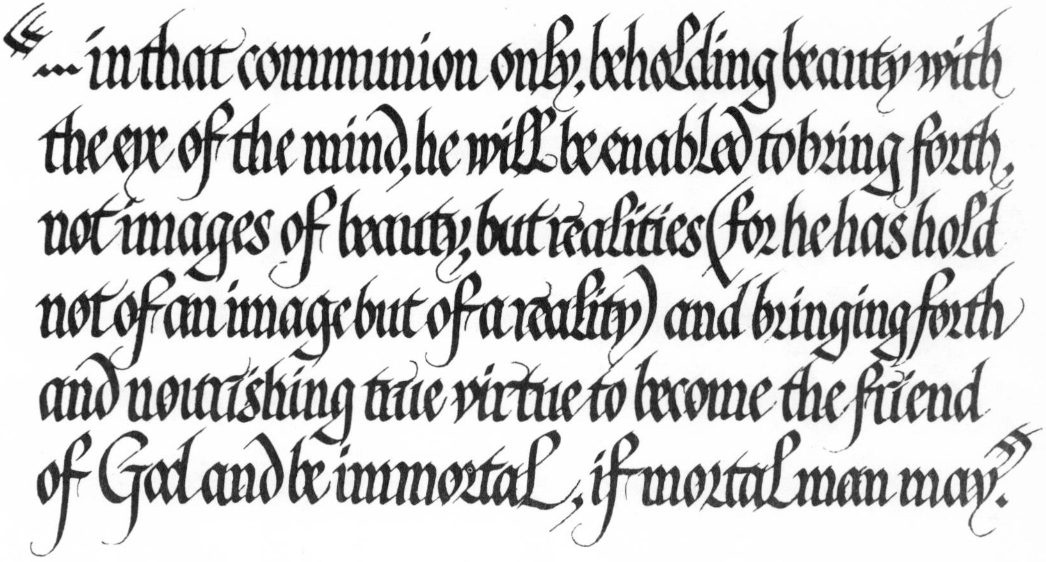

... in that communion only, beholding beauty with the eye of the mind, he will be enabled to bring forth, not images of beauty, but realities (for he has hold not of an image, but of a reality) and bringing forth and nourishing true virtue to become the friend of God and be immortal, if mortal man may.

Plate 73. Six lines from Plato. Part of an inscription on vellum written by Edward Johnston in April 1934. In the author's possession.

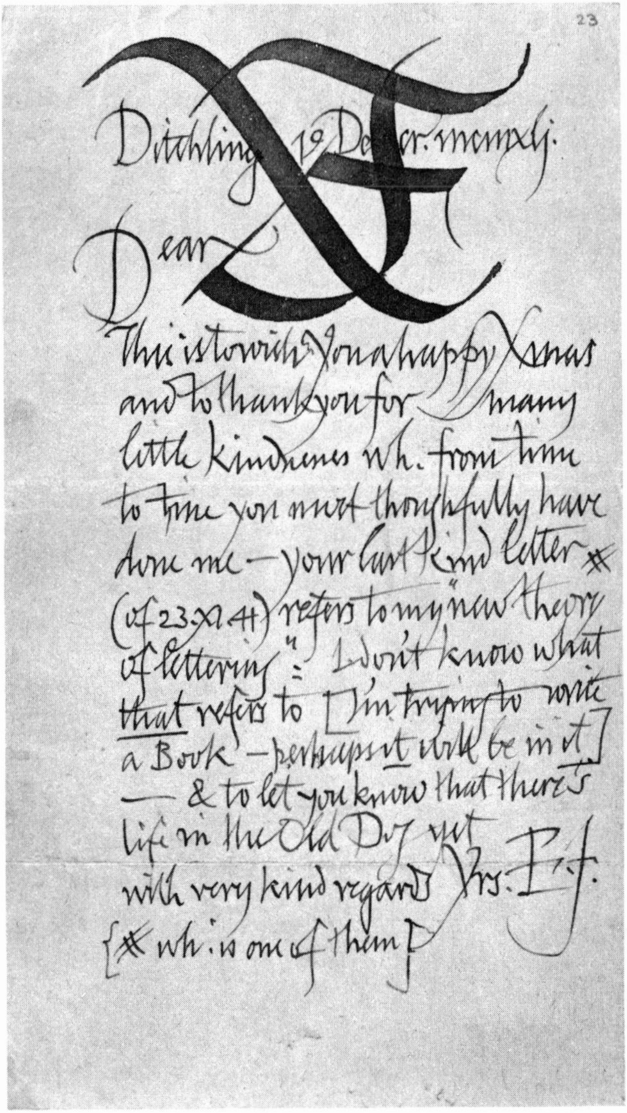

Plate 74. A letter written by Edward Johnston to the author on
19 December 1941. Bodleian Library, Oxford.

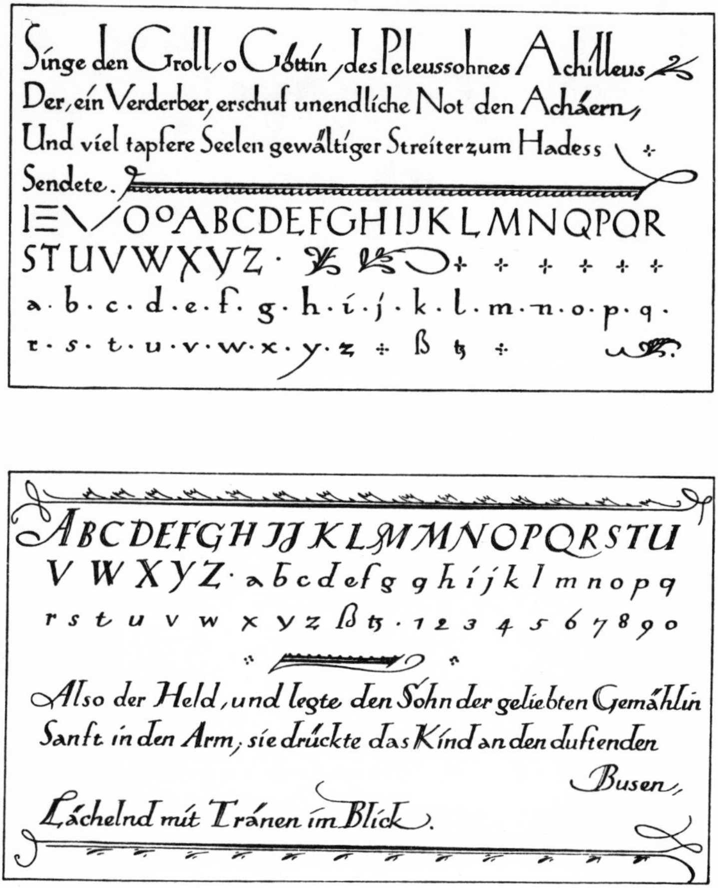

Plate 75. Roman and cursive scripts by Rudolf Koch. 1916.
(From *Rudolf Koch der Schreiber* by George Haupt.)

Observations
for Ingenious Penmen.
BY Mr. HART

T is hard a sprightly fancy to command
And give a Respit to the laboring Hand,
In vain we strive each trivial fault to hide
That shows but little Judgment, & more Pride.
Like some Nice Prude, offensive to the Sight
Exactness gives, at best, a Cold Delight.
Each painful stroke disgusts the lovely Mind,
For Art is lost, when Over-much refin'd.
To Err is Mortal, do whate'er we can,
Some faulty Trifles will confess the Man.
Wisest are they who each mad whim repress,
And shun Gross Errours, by committing less.

NON OMNIA POSSUMUS OMNES.

Plate 76. Poem by Mr Hart taken from George Bickham's *Universal Penman*, specially written for this book in a formal hand on vellum by Miss Margaret Alexander. 1951.

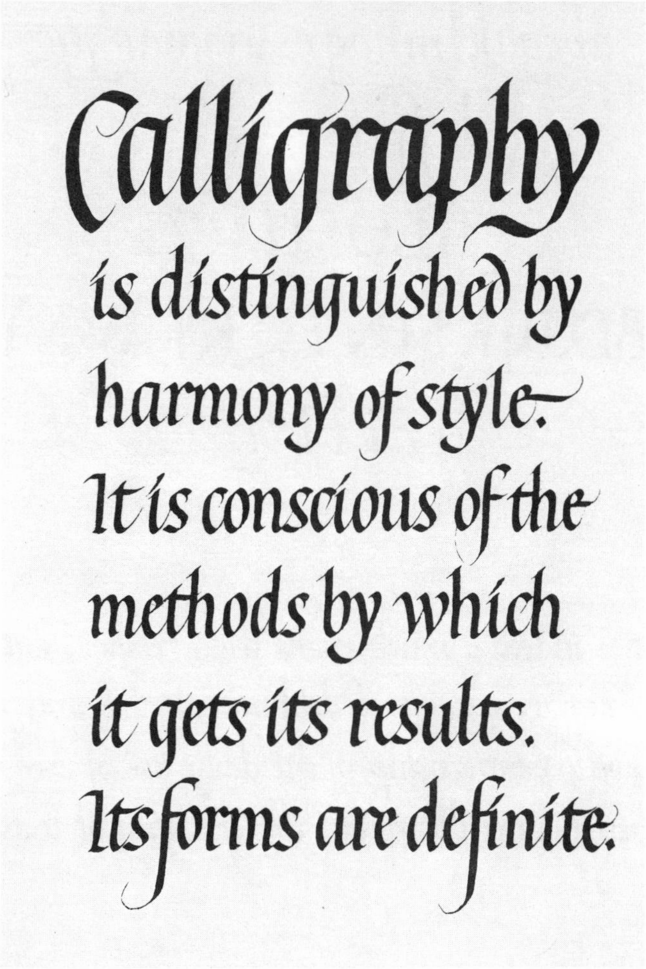

Calligraphy

is distinguished by harmony of style. It is conscious of the methods by which it gets its results. Its forms are definite.

Plate 77. Quotation from *Handwriting* by Professor E. A. Lowe, specially written for this book in a formal hand on vellum by Mrs Irene Wellington. 1951.

abcghklmnoqrsuvvwwyyz

deffijptxx

CEIJLOSUVZ

BDFGKMNPQRTWXY

AEFH?!

It is indeed a much more truly religious duty
to acquire a habit of deliberate, legible, and
lovely penmanship in the daily use of the
pen, than to illuminate any quantity of texts.

Plate 78. Examples from *Handwriting: Everyman's Handicraft*
by Graily Hewitt. Chiswick Press. 1916.

The most dangerous way in the World said they, is that which the Pilgrims go. They told me of the Slough of Despond, of the Wood & dark Mountains, of the Hill Difficulty, of the Lions, & also of the three Giants, moreover, that there was a foul Fiend haunted the Valley of Humiliation. Besides, said they, you must go over the Valley of the Shadow of Death, where the Light is Darkness. They told me also of Giant-Despair, of Doubting Castle & of the Ruins there. And did none of these things discourage you? No. They seemed but so many nothings to me. I still believed what Mr Telltrue had said, & that carried me beyond them all. John Bunyan 1628-1688

Plate 79. Page of *Writing and Writing Patterns*, Book V by Marion Richardson. University of London Press, 1935. Figure 8 is from the same source.

EXPLORING

On the fifteenth of July I began a careful survey of the island. I went up the creek first. After about two miles the tide did not flow any higher, and the stream was no more than a little brook. On its banks I found many pleasant meadows, covered with grass.

The next day I went up the same way again; and after going somewhat farther I found that the brook ceased, and the country became more woody than before. In this part I found melons on the ground and grape-vines spreading over the trees, with the clusters of grapes just now in their prime, very ripe and rich. I also saw an abundance of cocoa trees, as well as orange and lemon and citron trees.

['Robinson Crusoe']

Plate 80. Card No. 10 of *The Dryad Writing Cards* (originally named *The Barking Writing Cards*) by Alfred Fairbank. Dryad Press, Leicester, 1935.